HIDDEN IN BRUTAL DEVOTION

THE BRUTAL DUET BOOK 1

B J ALPHA

B J ALPHA

Copyright © 2023 by B J Alpha

All rights reserved.

No part of this book may be reproduced in any form or by any electronic or mechanical means, including information storage and retrieval systems, without written permission from the author, except for the use of brief quotations in a book review.

This book is a work of fiction. Characters, names, places and incidents are products of the authors imagination or used fictitiously.

Any similarity to actual events, locations or persons living or dead is purely coincidental.

Published by BJ Alpha

Edited by Cheyenne - Frogg Spa Editing

Proofread and edited by Dee Houpt

Cover Design by Haya In Designs

 Created with Vellum

DEDICATION

To all my readers who love smut this book is for you.
Oh and please read on to Book 2 because things are about to
get filthier.
Enjoy!
Love always BJ.

AUTHORS NOTE

WARNING: This book contains triggers. It has sensitive and explicit storylines such as graphic sexual scenes, violence, stalker tendencies, and strong language. It is recommended for readers aged eighteen and over.

HIDDEN IN BRUTAL DEVOTION

BJ ALPHA

PROLOGUE

Age Sixteen
Thalia

Martin's hand grazes my hip, and my body stiffens under his touch. My eyes snap up to him as he opens the kitchen cupboard above my head, only to find him staring down at me with hunger in his eyes. He licks his lips, the motion sending a sickening tremble through my body. I take a step back, desperate to break any connection, his lecherous stare filling me with trepidation. My skin crawls when his eyes latch on to my T-shirt, as though he was seeing through the baggy gray material straight at my boobs. I even put a camisole on beneath the T-shirt, hoping to hide my generous bust.

Just as he steps closer toward me, the kitchen door swings open, and Jace steps into the room, instantly spotting Martin. The swelling around the shiner he has looks worse today, and the undercurrent of tension between them heightens even further. I grab my glass of water and step around the counter so I'm nowhere near

Martin, the tension between the two of them still at boiling point. I register Jace's fists clench and unclench beside him, his jaw tics, and his muscular body tightens with anger.

I swallow past the lump in my throat, knowing I need to dispel the atmosphere and quickly. The last thing we need is Jace to screw up his future—not when he has so much riding on it and when he's so close to leaving. I ignore the flutter of nervousness in my stomach at the thought of him leaving—without me. He needs to do this. For us. It's our only hope.

I take a step toward him, but he doesn't even register me. No, his eyes are set firmly on the asshole behind me, our foster father.

My gaze roams over Jace's body. His basketball shorts hang low, showing a defined V, he's shirtless as usual, and I want nothing more than to trail my fingertips over each and every firm ridge. His dark hair is a ruffled mess, and his olive skin is still damp from the shower.

Jace glances down toward me. "Go to your room, Thalia." Then, he darts his attention back toward Martin. There's no way I'm leaving him here, not with the tension in the room, not with Martin antagonizing him like this in a silent stare-off.

"I need your help with my math homework," I lie, trailing a finger down his arm. A trail of goose bumps follows my finger, and he shuffles from side to side, his shoulders easing at my touch.

He exhales. "Come on." Jace places his hand on the lower part of my back and guides me toward my room.

2

Slamming the door shut behind us, we're finally in our safe haven. I can finally relax.

"I hate him," he spits out.

"I know, me too." I drag the T-shirt over my head and throw it to the floor.

Jace's eyes linger on my exposed chest before he glances away, and he flops down onto my bed with an arm tucked behind his head. "So, what do you need my help with?"

How about you? I bite my lip on my snarky comeback and lie down beside him. "I lied." I stare into his black eyes, his gaze holding mine.

He chuckles. "Of course you fucking did."

He knows I saved his ass tonight; Martin is just waiting for an excuse to call the cops on him and destroy his future. Our future.

Jace dips his head, and his soft lips find mine. I open my mouth, allowing his tongue to sweep in. His kiss is slow and gentle, calculated, and his large palm trails over my stomach, inching my camisole higher with each movement. "You're so fucking beautiful."

I hold the nape of his neck and pull him back to me, moaning into his mouth. "Fuck." His heart is hammering against mine as our kiss becomes frantic.

"Please," I beg.

Jace stops kissing me and pulls back, his eyes searching mine. He rests his forehead against mine.

He licks his lips. "I wanna . . ." His throat bobs, and he trembles under my touch. He's nervous. "Can I taste you?" His eyes flick down, and my face flushes at his words. He wants to taste me down there. This is new to us—both of us—and I can't wait.

I nod, and a thrill of excitement thrums through my veins as he sits back on his heels and lowers my sleep shorts and panties in one motion. His eyes are so dark, I can't make out his pupils at all now.

Jace stares down at my pussy, and I move to close my legs, feeling slightly embarrassed, but he forces my thighs open wider. "Don't hide from me, Thalia. This is my pussy, you understand me?"

I choke on air at his words, then without warning, he dips down, and his tongue flicks over my hole and up to my clit. A whimper escapes my lips, and I grip Jace's hair, determined to keep him there where it feels so good.

My heels dig into the mattress with each sweep of his tongue, while his dark eyes find mine. Heavy with lust, he watches me writhe under every motion of that amazing mouth of his. "Oh god, Jace."

I don't know what has come over me, but I drag down the straps of my top and release my tits. His eyes bug out when I squeeze them between the palms of my hands.

"Holy fuck, Thalia," he exhales deeply on a moan. His grip on my thighs tightens to the point of pain, but I don't stop. I play and squeeze and pinch my tits, knowing I'm driving him mad.

Jace groans into my pussy, completely devouring me, and when he begins to thrust against the mattress, a wave of wetness leaks from me, but he laps at it, pushing his face harder into my pussy.

"Fuck, I can't. I can't get enough of this pussy, Thalia.

Your taste drives me fucking wild." His tongue curls and dives into my hole as he pushes me further and further toward my climax.

My hips rise off the bed to meet his face, and the moment he sucks on my clit, I'm gone. I throw my head back and scream, "Holy shit. Yes, yes. Yes!"

Jace ruts against the bed, moaning and panting, and just knowing he's so turned on both excites and reassures me of our relationship.

I slowly come down from my orgasm, my chest rising and falling. Who knew something could feel so good? Jace has brought me to orgasm with his fingers before, but this? This is something else.

He sits up, his mouth open in awe, the wetness on his chin evidence of my arousal. "Fuck, Thalia. You're like a fucking porn star."

I scrunch up my nose at his analogy, making him chuckle, before his gaze turns heated. "Seriously, though, I nearly fucking came from licking your sweet pussy."

I bite on my lip. "Jace?" He sweeps his arm across his mouth. "I want to have sex with you." My heart hammers in my chest, waiting for his rejection. We've been fooling around for months, but Jace has been adamant that we don't have sex.

At first, I thought it was because he was getting it elsewhere, so he didn't need me for that, but now I know it's because he's scared if we do it, I won't want him to leave. That I'll become so attached, I'll beg him not to go. I can't help but hope it's him who's worried about becoming attached, that it's him who won't want to leave.

"Please?"

I slide my hand down to my pussy and swirl my finger around my clit, and his eyes bug out before darting back up to mine. "Fucking killing me here, Thalia." His words are choked as he strokes his hand over his covered cock.

"I know. I want to, though," I pout. For so many reasons, I want to. I want him to be my first, I want to be his first.

When he goes off to college tomorrow, I want him to think of me—only me—and then there's the other reason, the one I don't want to think about, so I shove it as far back in my mind as I possibly can, where all the other thoughts go when it comes to that.

Jace pushes down his shorts and takes out his wallet, retrieving a condom. I sit up on my elbows and watch as he rolls it down his solid cock. "Carl gave it to me. I haven't . . ." His words trail off when I pull his lips to mine. I know he hasn't slept with anyone before; I don't need him to explain to me again.

He's between my legs rubbing his cock around my hole. "It's going to hurt a bit, Thalia." His concerned eyes meet mine.

I force the lump in my throat down. "I know, I want this. I want you, Jace." Our eyes lock as he pushes inside me slowly, and I grimace a little at the bite of pain.

"Shit, you're really tight." His mouth is open, as though he's astounded, and he slowly pushes in a little more before stopping. "Are you okay?"

I'm already worried he's going to back out with the concern visibly etched on his face. I nod and bite my lip, trailing my hand over his jaw. I bring his face toward mine, knowing what I need to do. "I like you stretching me, Jace."

"Oh fuck, I love how dirty you are."

He pushes in more, then he pulls almost all the way out before slamming in and past the barrier that was between us. My back arches off the bed with a wince.

"Oh fuck. I'm in. I'm in, baby." He pulls back and pushes in again.

"More. More, Jace." I dig my nails into his back, determined to leave my mark on him.

His lips meet mine, and his tongue clashes with my own. We kiss frantically as he pushes in and out of me.

"Oh fuck, I think—" He pulls back to look at me, his eyes wide in panic. "Shit, I'm . . ." He drops his head into the crook of my neck as I feel him swell inside me.

I hold him there as tight as I possibly can; I hold Jace Matthews in my arms, wishing the night to never end, because tomorrow? That's when reality sets in, that's when my hell begins. I feel it brewing, and if truth be told, Jace can too, he's just choosing to ignore it.

My eyes well with tears.

"I love you, Thalia. Wait for me, and I'll wait for you."

I want to believe him; I want to believe those words he whispers so tenderly into my ear as his lips dust over my neck.

"I'll wait for you. There's only ever going to be you."

He nods into my hair, believing every word from my traitorous mouth.

The truth will only destroy him. Him and his dream.

Him and us.

ONE

F ive years later ...

Cole

I scan the crowded floor. My cock is already pumping at the thought of the action it's going to get tonight. I lock on to the two giggly brunettes eyeing me like a piece of steak; they know I'm mignon, the finest steak you can get. You only have to look at me to know that. I'm stacked—real fucking stacked—I have the natural golden complexion women love and a smile to make them open their legs without me asking. Yep, finish it off with a cock men would die for, and I'm the epitome of every woman's wet dream. Men too, I'm guessing.

I give the girls a wink, and they practically swoon. *Mmm, too easy.* I'll come back to them if nothing else takes my fancy.

My eyes lock on to a girl behind the bar throwing her head back with a loud, rambunctious laugh that makes me chuckle. I'm used to girls that giggle or fake a laugh, not the loud belly laughing, not the natural shit this girl is letting out. Her laugh is infectious. I watch as she smacks the ass of one of the bartenders with a towel.

My eyes trail down her body. Fuck me sideways, she's hot. She has curves, real fucking curves, not that fake shit I have to contend with. Her tits are heavy and straining against her camisole, her plump lips are glossy, and I already imagine that gloss on my cock. Over it, all around it. My dick leaks a little, hungry for the girl's glossy lips. She has hips and an ass for me to grab hold of and fuck every way I like without worrying she's going to snap if I fuck her too hard. Her blonde hair trails down her back in loose waves, almost touching that fine ass tucked tightly into jean shorts. Hell yeah, perfect length to wrap around my fist while I fuck her hard.

I push off the balcony railing and make my way over toward the bar, and as if by some magnetic force, her eyes draw up and meet mine. She licks those plump lips, and I can't help but smirk when I consider my earlier analogy of me being a piece of steak, because fuck me, does she look like she wants to devour me.

"Hello, beautiful."

She exhales in annoyance at my words, her shoulders slacken, and she rolls her eyes with attitude. *What the fuck?*

Miss Attitude stands before me with her arms crossed over her chest, pushing those banging beauties up higher and forcing my cock to throb harder. She narrows her blue eyes at me, as though she knows my cock wants to spurt on her tits, her lips, and—fuck me—that gorgeous pissed-off face too.

"Are you even listening to me?"

I jolt at her words. Am I? I'm currently pussytized by her.

"Huh?"

"I said. What. Would. You. Like. To. Drink?" She punctuates each word as though I'm dumb.

I drag my tongue slowly over my bottom lip; her eyes latch on to the piercing, and I swear to fucking St. Chris on the cross, her nipples pucker. Game-fucking-on, beauty.

"I'll have a Balls Deep." I smirk as her eyes widen at my response before her face contorts in disgust. She opens her mouth, no doubt to spiel a load of shit at me, but I shake my head and point to the sign on the counter. The one that reads *Cocktail of the day: Balls Deep*.

"You're a real joker, aren't you?"

My little beauty starts gathering cocktail shit together, and her tits and ass swing as she shakes the cocktail thing.

"I try." I shrug cockily.

"Well, Casanova, if you're wanting to get balls deep, those two little leggy brunettes over there are interested." She turns and points over my shoulder, and I glance at where she's pointing. Sure enough, the two brunettes from earlier give me an eager wave. I fake a smile and turn back toward my little beauty.

"Not interested."

She places the drink down in front of me. "That'll be ten dollars."

"For a Balls Deep? That's cheap, beauty." I throw a twenty on the counter. "Keep the change for a tip."

She goes over to the till, swaps the money over, and

stuffs the change into the tip jar. "Thank you," she throws over her shoulder as I watch her ass sway as she walks toward the next customer.

I spend the next four drinks watching her flirt up a fucking storm with asshole after asshole, but me? She narrows her eyes at me like she despises me. My jaw tics in annoyance. Never in my fucking life have I had to try so hard for attention. I cast another look over my shoulder, and the two brunettes wave toward me again like a pair of fucking puppets. They're eagerly waiting for me, guaranteed balls deep in both of them. I look back toward my beauty to find her staring at me. Interesting. Maybe she's not as unaffected after all.

"You see something you like?" I smirk at her knowingly.

She leans closer, and I actually think she's going to kiss me; I can virtually taste that gum she chewed only ten minutes ago. Her soft lips brush my cheek, and if I were to turn just slightly—

"Actually, I do." She snatches the twenty out of my hand and marches off toward the till. "Although, I prefer fifties, for future reference." She smiles back at me, and I wanna spank that sassy ass so bad. I grin into my drink, imagining all the positions we could try that in.

TIA

I stick the change into the tip jar. This poor dude has single-handedly filled the jar tonight. One step closer to my goal, I can't help but grin to myself.

"What time do you get off, beauty?"

I dry the glass and place it back on the shelf. "My name's not beauty." I feign annoyance, when in reality, I'm quietly thrilled I'm being called something other than *woman*, *bitch*, *buttercup*. I shudder at the latter, determined to keep the memories at bay.

"What's your name, then?" He smiles into his drink as his eyes rove over my body for the hundredth time tonight.

Whereas sometimes I can get angsty at a man's attention, for some reason, the moment our eyes connected, I felt a warmth toward this guy that I can't explain. His fun-loving attitude appeals to me. As much as I realize he's clearly a player, I can't help but find myself attracted to the bona fide Casanova.

"Tia. My name's Tia."

His Adam's apple slowly bobs in his throat as he takes another carefully orchestrated drink of his beer. He swapped them out from cocktails over an hour ago.

"I'm Cole, nice to meet you." He holds out his hand for me to shake, and the action stuns me a little. His bright-green eyes twinkle with mischief and amusement at my lack of response, making him nod toward his hand. I drop the towel on the counter and place my hand in his.

The moment we connect, my heart jumps in my chest, causing me to gasp for air. His touch is like a shock to my racing heart, forcing me to learn how to breathe once again. Cole's firm hand grips mine. His hand is so large, it engulfs my much smaller one. A feeling of both protectiveness and possession swirl through me, my eyes connect with his, and he narrows his as though confused by what appears to be a mutual feeling.

His eyes shimmer under the strobe lights, but I don't miss the look of hunger behind them, an undercurrent of desire shooting between us. I've never felt so enamored by a simple touch, so alive. My heart misses a beat again.

"You're coming home with me tonight, Tia." His eyes stay locked on mine with no room for negotiation but still awaiting a reaction from me, waiting for an acknowledgment of his words.

I swallow and give him a small nod, my body taking over my mind.

"I'm going to show you exactly what it means to be balls deep, beauty." He winks as he releases my hand, and I stand there, stunned to the spot.

Just what the hell have I gotten myself into now?

CHAPTER
TWO

C ole

We crash through the penthouse doors, her legs locked around my thick waist. I suck at the skin on the side of her neck, trailing kisses over the aggressive bite marks to dull away the sting. The taste of her coconut lotion fills my mouth, and I practically salivate for more. My grip on her ass tightens as I grind into her against the door.

She's like a fucking wildcat, clawing at me, moaning in my ear, "Please. Cole, you need to fuck me."

When I tugged her into the taxi and my lips crashed against hers, we were instantly inseparable. Straddling me, she rocked her tight little ass over my rock-hard cock, and I had to concentrate real fucking hard not to come on the spot.

Tia nips at my ear, then licks down my jawline before her tongue clashes with mine once again. She sucks my pierced tongue into her mouth, toying with the barbell.

Her nipples poke through her top, causing me to groan when they graze over my chest.

"Fuck, beauty. I need that tongue round my cock so bad."

"Mmm, I want to taste you." Her moans vibrate over my neck as she flicks her tongue over mine.

Tia drops to her knees and opens her mouth wide.

"Fucking Jesus, Tia. You look so goddamn incredible on your knees for me." I unbuckle my belt, and her blue eyes flare with desire.

Slowly popping open the buttons of my jeans, I don't break eye contact. My heart races to fuck her mouth hard and quick, but my mind wills me to slow the hell down and savor every minute, because something tells me I'll never get enough of this girl. Never.

I pull my cock from my boxers, and her eyes bulge when she sees the piercing.

"You ever been with a guy with his cock pierced?"

She shakes her head from side to side.

"Kiss it, beauty." I bring my cock to her glossy lips and let out a hiss when she swirls her tongue around my Prince Albert piercing before sucking on the end tenderly, the sensation shooting to my balls.

"Oh fuck." My fists clench by my side as I'm eager to ram my cock into her.

I step forward, giving her no option but to take more of me. Her eyes remain locked on mine, bringing with it an immeasurable amount of sexual tension, but something strange also passes between us. A connection, one that makes my pulse race faster and causes my heart to beat profusely. Tenderly, I stroke my hand down her cheek, the tip of my cock sitting in her mouth. I can't take it anymore, fuck. I plunge forward, my eyes closing when the soft wetness of her mouth engulfs my cock. Forcing it to the back of her throat, she groans in ecstasy.

Holy shit, that's good.

My hand goes to the back of her head, and I push her toward my cock until her nose is flush against my trimmed hair, and the feel of the air escaping her nostrils causes a shiver down my spine. I throw my head back, and my mouth drops open when I start fucking her mouth like a madman. Gone is the need to be slow, gone are any thoughts of savoring every moment. No, I need her now. I need her choking on my cock and my cum flowing from her hungry lips.

"Take it," I choke out when I lodge myself down her throat even further. Her lack of gag reflex is uncommon and absolutely incredible. My hands tangle in her hair, fisting it to the point of pain. But I'm beyond caring. All I want is my cock satisfied by her fucking incredible mouth.

"Take all my thick cock, beauty." I grip her hair harder. Her tongue continues to swirl around my cock when there must be barely any room in her mouth for it to move. The thought sends a tingle to my balls, and as if reading my mind, her hand moves to my ball sack, giving them a gentle tug. Her drool mixes with her palm, and the wetness is in-fucking-credible.

I drop my head to stare at her heavy eyes and her mouth stuffed with my cock. Fuck me, she's gorgeous. I ram in again, the telltale sign of my cum about to spurt. "Fuck, beauty. Don't stop, fucking don't stop."

My mouth drops open as my cum spurts down her throat. I cling to her head to stablize my footing, my whole fucking body shaking with the power of my release.

My chest rises and falls rapidly as I stare down in wonder at the only woman who has managed to make me feel like this, ever. Her eyes don't leave mine, and hers soften slightly as I tenderly stroke the hair from her cheek.

There's something there, something I can't put my finger on, a vulnerability, a need to keep her, protect her. I realize in this moment that she's the girl for me, the one you hear people talk about, the one you never want to get away.

I slowly withdraw my cock from her mouth. I'm still hard. She sucked my soul from my body, and yet, I'm still hard. I get the feeling I'll never get enough of her.

She swallows, and I watch the motion. Loving the fact she's probably still swallowing my cum, still tasting me on her tongue, my cock jerks in response to my thoughts, and a small smile plays on her lips.

"Are you going to show me what you can do with that?" She motions with a nod toward my cock, and I grin back at her.

"Beauty, I'm about to hammer you so hard, you're gonna need fixing back together." I smirk and raise my eyebrow in jest.

I hold out my hand, and Tia rises to her feet. "Less talk, more action, big boy." She pats me on my chest, but I grip her hand, holding it on my chest, letting her feel my racing heartbeat, feel the connection.

She licks her lips and swallows. Her eyes dart away from mine, as though she's trying to break the connection between us, refusing to acknowledge the spark we both know is there. I let her, for now.

Bending down, I take hold of her from underneath her knees, throw her over my shoulder, and stride into the bedroom.

"Oh my god, Cole." She laughs, causing me to chuckle to myself.

"Gonna nail you to my bed."

"I'd like to see you try!" she jokes back.

"Oh, I'm gonna." I throw her down onto the bed, causing her to bounce with a giggle. She brushes the hair from her face and leans up on her elbows. "Now, you gonna undress, or have I got to do it for you?" I quirk a brow at her playfully.

She nibbles on her lip to stop herself from laughing. "I'll do it, big boy."

With a smug smile on her face, she lifts her top over her head, exposing her bare chest. I don't know whether to be enamored at her gorgeous tits or pissed she's not wearing a bra.

She brings her hand to her nipples, and, fuck me, I'm done.

TIA

Cole stumbles as he tries to rush and take his jeans off. I watch on as he lowers his boxers over his thick thighs. Jesus, the man is built.

When I saw the piercing, I had to do a double take, and his smooth thick cock was gorgeous. As soon as I tasted him, I wanted more. His thickness was more than I'd experienced before, and from the look Cole was giving me, he was in awe of how much I was managing to take. All of it. Every thick, smooth inch of it.

Nothing like a good blow job to drain all coherent thoughts from a man's brain. I think I sucked every thought out of him.

The way he looked at me was unexpected; it sent a tremble through my body because the only other person who had ever looked at me with such admiration had broken my heart, and I was determined for that look to never happen again.

Cole climbs onto the bed, already jerking his thick cock in his big hand. His chest is golden and clean of any marks, and he's well-groomed, not the usual rugged guy I would go for. His smile is wide with a hint of mischief that no doubt has gotten him out of trouble over the years, and the thought makes me smile as I imagine his personality: cocky but fun loving.

"You're so beautiful when you smile. Your whole face lights up."

I blush under his compliment and turn my head away, instead choosing to shimmy out of my jean shorts. My red G-string is soaked, and it's a welcome reprieve when I toss it to the floor.

Cole situates himself between my open thighs, and he brushes over my tit, caressing it gently before working up toward my throat, where his fingers tighten ever so slightly. I lick my lips, waiting to see what he does next. His lips crash down onto mine, and his tongue flicks mine as we fight for control of the kiss. He rubs his cock over my wet pussy, and I can't help the moan escaping my lips.

"Fuck, that's it, moan for my cock." His words brush over my lips. Slowly, he slips inside me, stretching my pussy inch by inch. "Fuck, you feel so damn good, beauty."

My body stills, and on instinct, Cole's does too, sensing my unease.

"Con . . . condom, Cole." I pat his chest, panic racing through me. "Condom."

His lips tug up into a smile. "Don't fuckin panic, beauty. I'm clean. Are you on birth control?"

My eyebrows furrow. He's clean? His lips graze mine,

earning a moan from me and causing my pussy to clench.

"Are you?" he prompts, still not moving.

"Yes." The word comes out on a stuttered breath.

Cole nods with a coy smile and a sharp nip to my lip. "I've never fucked without one." He draws back to stare into my eyes, his words seeping into me. This means something to him; he's asking for my permission, and for the first time in my life, I want to give it. A small nod makes his eyes flare, and his body pulls back before he slams into me, making the wooden bedposts smack against the wall.

"Thank fuck, beauty." He pulls back. "Thank fuck."

Slam!

"More." I beg as my heart races and my pussy clenches, pulling him in with each slam from his strong body, each grind of his heavy hips.

Cole's piercing hits me each and every time as he angles himself just right, sending a wave of euphoria through me and a gush of wetness out of me. "Oh god, Cole. Don't stop."

The bed knocks against the wall with each slam, each purposeful, strong thrust.

"Fucking gorgeous, beauty." His eyes close, and he bites the inside of his mouth. "Shit."

I moan, knowing he's close, knowing he's losing control. I squeeze him tighter, using my muscles to milk him while moving my hands toward my nipples. I pinch them, the sensation vibrating through my body. The look of pure lust on Cole's face and that delicious piercing hitting me perfectly is enough to tip me over the edge. My eyes lock with Cole's.

I tighten around him; my hands squeeze at my tits, the key on the necklace I wear falls between them, and I come with his eyes flicking between my tits and my face.

"Fuuuuuuuck, beauty." He slams into me once more, and his cock swells. Then, I feel his release.

His hips snap back and forth, back and forth, emptying every drop of his cum inside me before he drops onto his elbows, grabs ahold of me, and rolls so I'm lying on top of him with his cock still stuffed inside me. His large palm strokes my hair affectionately, and I revel under his gentle touch.

"That was incredible, beauty."

I lift my head to stare into his emerald orbs. "It was, wasn't it?"

A cocky smile tugs at his lips. "Gimme five, and I'll be ready for round two."

His eyebrows dance with a wiggle, causing me to chuckle. "You better. I'm still waiting to be nailed," I snark back at him.

Cole bites his bottom lip. "I meant it, you know." His tone turns serious. "I've never not used one." His eyes stay locked on mine, the truth seeping from them. I nod at his words. "You're special, beauty. I can see it; I can see you." His Adam's apple bobs as his fingers graze almost lovingly over my chin.

My eyes well with tears, unsure of how to react, unsure of the sense of vulnerability washing over me. My lips part to tell him to stop, to tell him . . .

But he shakes his head and leans forward, gently

24

pressing his lips to mine. My heart freefalls, and my body trembles under his gentle touch.

I've never felt so special—so treasured—in my entire life.

Apart from that one time.

I close my eyes and give myself over to the feel of Cole's hard body below me, inside me, consuming me, and I relish in it.

THREE

—╬—

C ole
   I turn over and stretch my arm out to scoop up my beauty, only to find the space beside me empty. Rising up on my elbows, I stare toward the bathroom door in confusion, searching for some sort of sound or clue as to where she might be.

Maybe she's in the lounge area? I throw the covers off and ignore my junk swaying as I fly toward the door. Surely she didn't leave, right?

The lounge is empty, and now I'm pissed. Scanning the bedroom floor, I see all her belongings are gone, she's gone. I grind my teeth in annoyance.

Grabbing my phone from the nightstand, I dial the number I know can get me answers, because, boy, do I want answers.

Did she not understand when I told her she was special?

"What's wrong?" My brother's voice fills the room.

"Lucas, I lost something. Someone."

"Fuck. Was there trouble?"

I scrub a hand through my cropped hair. "No, it was after the fight. I went to that club you mentioned, Envy, and I hooked up with a girl."

Lucas scoffs. "Of course you fucking did."

I roll my eyes at my brother's response. Just because he doesn't do random sex, he thinks it's okay to have an opinion on my choices. Well, screw that.

"I don't need your opinion, asshat. It's *my* dick!"

"Yeah, probably riddled with all sorts of shit."

My mind wanders back to Tia. I wasn't lying when I said I've never not used a condom. I've always wrapped it before I tapped it. But with her, it was different, *she* was different. There was a spark, an energy, a connection between us that wasn't just sexual. Maybe it's my lack of relationship experience to feel this way, but I know deep down, something is telling me she's mine.

"I want you to find her for me."

"Why?"

"Because I like her." I swallow away the vulnerability I feel. The first fucking girl I feel something for, and she left. In fact, scrap that, she didn't just leave, she practically ran.

"You like her," Lucas mimics sarcastically. He's always like this; he doesn't understand my need and sexual appetite, therefore, anything to do with the opposite sex, he admonishes.

I swallow away the panic trying to escape me, the silence between me and Lucas filling the room.

"What do you know about her?"

My shoulders ease slightly, knowing he's going to help.

"Her name's Tia. She works at the back of the bar."

"Should be easy enough to find. Gimme twenty minutes; I'll do a quick search and send you an address over."

My muscles sag in relief. "Thanks."

"Oh, and Cole? Rage wants you to check the gym out too."

My jaw locks in frustration. Of course he does.

"Sure," I clip back, ending the call and throwing my phone onto the bed.

When I first agreed to come to Basington, Ocean City, I was told it would be for the night. Now, it's turning out to be a fucking week. I have my own mixed martial arts gym to run, never mind checking out all of Lucas's and Rage's business ventures. Their scheme to grow the business is commendable, but all I want to do is assist with training our guys. Throw in a few fights every now and again, and I'm one hell of a happy guy. Especially when the gym bunnies want my cock.

What more can a guy want?

I scrub the towel through my damp hair and pick up my phone. Lucas came through as promised, and I grin to myself as I open the attached document.

Tia's blue eyes gleam back at me, causing my heart to jackhammer in my chest. Fuck me, she's beautiful.

I read her credentials; Tia Jones, age twenty-one,

lives at Cavendish Court, apartment 52, Basington, New Jersey.

She works as a part-time server at a local diner during the day and as a bartender at night at Club Envy.

Lucas also sent over her hours of work, so I know today she has a rest day. Perfect.

I scan over the additional information, reading that Tia also studies an online college course in art, specifically children's illustrations. *Mmm, so my girl is good at drawing.*

Opening my closet, I pull out a plain white T-shirt and tug on a pair of jeans. I smile to myself as I imagine Tia's face when she sees me at her apartment.

It's time to go get my beauty.

TIA

I drag my comb through my hair. After leaving the penthouse before Cole woke this morning to avoid any awkward silence, I came home, tidied round, and showered.

A knock at my apartment door causes me to sigh. Knowing it's probably the old lady from down the hall again, I plaster on a smile and swing my door open. But it's not her, nope, because standing in front of me with a huge cheeky smile is the guy that I kissed goodbye only a few hours ago. Cole.

My eyes must bug out because he chuckles, saying, "Beauty, if you don't close your mouth, I'm going to have to stuff it full of cock. You're already giving me a semi, standing there with your tits on display."

I snap my mouth closed and trail my eyes down my body. I have a long rock band T-shirt on, sans bra because I just showered.

I stare back at Cole. He's leaning against the door-frame, looking freshly showered. He wears a tight white

T-shirt that showcases his huge chest and biceps, jeans that stretch over his thick muscular thighs, and chunky unlaced boots. He smells incredible—his cologne lingers in the air—so much so, I find myself wanting to lean in and smell his neck, trailing a long lick all the way down to . . .

Wow, his dick really *is* hard.

Cole clears his throat. "As much as I'd appreciate you eating me for breakfast, I actually brought it with me." He holds two brown paper bags up in front of me and then proceeds to push past me, welcoming himself into my apartment.

A chuckle makes me turn toward the small living space to see Cole unpacking the contents of the brown bags onto the small kitchen countertop.

Realizing I'm still standing like an idiot in shock with the door wide open, I slam it shut and cross my arms over my chest and walk toward the kitchen.

"Cole, what are you doing here?"

Cole's face drops, and he stops what he's doing, making me feel guilty at the look of vulnerability in his eyes. They search mine, but I'm not sure what he's looking for.

He clears his throat and continues unpacking the food. "I brought breakfast, beauty. With you running out on me so quick, I didn't get the chance to feed you." His eyes snap back up toward mine accusingly.

I shift from foot to foot uncomfortably, tugging on the hem of the T-shirt. His eyes follow my movement, causing heat to creep up my neck and into my cheeks.

"Gotta say, I've never had a woman run out on me in

the morning," he jokes to lighten the mood.

I straighten my back and walk over to the small two-seater table. Pulling out a chair, I take a seat. "There's a first time for everything," I snark back, trying to act unfazed by his presence.

Cole chuckles. "That there is." He picks up the breakfast items and brings them over to the table. Bending down, he tucks a strand of my damp hair behind my ear. "And I told you last night, I had a first time with you."

My gaze meets Cole's when he pulls the chair out and takes a seat, dwarfing it in the process. He angles himself to face me. "I didn't use protection, beauty. That's not something I've done before." I swallow at his words. "When I said you were special, I meant it. You're not the type of girl I want leaving my bed in the morning." Cole laughs to himself while brushing a hand over his buzz cut. Appearing slightly uncomfortable, he glances away and exhales before his eyes meet mine once again. "Pretty sure I'd never want you to leave my bed. You get me?"

I stare at him in disbelief. I'm pretty sure Cole just told me he wants me?

"I want you, beauty. In my bed, on my cock, and, more importantly"—he taps his hand over his heart—"in here."

I suck in a sharp breath and a tremor works through my body at the sheer look of sincerity behind his words.

"I don't even know you," I say, my voice a delicate whisper.

Cole's face breaks out into his wide signature grin. "Then, let's get to know each other."

CHAPTER
FOUR

C ole

Tia breaks off another piece of the banana muffin I brought over and places it into her mouth. Just seeing her little tongue dart out brings a wave of emotion over me. The thought of her tongue around my cock, again in my mouth, and over my piercings makes my cock jump in my jeans and pre-cum leak from the tip. I shift in my chair and try not to think of all the fucking we did last night and into this morning.

So far, Tia hasn't told me anything I don't already know. So, I'm desperate to delve a little deeper into my beauty.

"What do you do for fun?" I ask her with a wiggle of my eyebrows.

She throws a muffin wrapper at my head, making me chuckle. "I don't make a habit of going home with charming muscled men, that's for sure."

"You think I'm charming?" I grin at her.

She rolls her eyes in jest. "You know you are."

I grin back at her knowingly.

"I like to draw." She nibbles her lip almost nervously, waiting for a reaction.

"Draw?"

Tia nods.

"You going to show me what you draw?"

She smiles at my words, making me wonder if anybody has ever seen her drawings before. Seen her.

"I have a whole portfolio I can show you after breakfast?" Her expectant eyes hold mine, causing my heart to constrict at her vulnerability over her work-manship.

Hell, she could draw fucking stick men and I'd tell her they were incredible. Preferably stick men fucking, but I'm not sure how that works.

Something tells me Tia needs approval, and I'm all for giving approval.

"Fuck yeah, beauty."

She blushes and darts her eyes away. "How about you? What do you like to do?"

I smile back at my girl. "Fight. I like to fight."

Her eyebrows rise. "Fight?"

"Yep. Me and my brothers own a bunch of fight clubs, gyms. I help train the current fighters while my brothers work more behind the scenes."

She flicks her gaze over my body, and I almost push out my chest in pride at her perusal. "Makes sense, you're . . . solid."

I throw my head back on a laugh. "Damn fucking right I'm solid." I blatantly adjust my rock-hard cock, making Tia laugh.

"Tell me about your family." She smiles as she takes another sip of the fresh orange juice I bought for her.

"So, I was brought up by my nana. My parents passed away when I was a kid." I swallow back the emotion discussing my parents always brings up. "My mom died during childbirth, and my dad drank himself to death," I tack on.

Tia's eyes melt with sympathy, and her hand settles over mine. The comforting gesture makes me turn her hand over and take a hold of it, threading our fingers together. The feeling is foreign to me, but at the same time, it feels natural with her. "Anyway, my nana, she fostered kids. When I was eight, she took on my brother Lucas. He'd been through a hellish childhood. He was withdrawn and a total dick, but she helped pull him out of his shell. Don't get me wrong, he doesn't let anyone see the real him, but I do, and I know my brother Rage does too."

"Your nana sounds incredible."

Tia's soft smile gives me the determination to carry on. "She died three years ago. She left us with enough money for us to pay off the loan we took out on our first fight club. Rage is, like, incredible with accounts and shit, and Lucas has a total business head with so much intensity behind him, he makes business deals with ease." I chuckle at my analogy of Lucas. The clowns he works alongside to get sponsors for our fighters think his whole serious and brash demeanor is purely business. If they fucking knew the guy was like that twenty-four-seven, they'd have him committed.

I take a gulp of my smoothie before wiping my

mouth with the back of my hand, keeping the other firmly locked around Tia's. "So, have you always lived in Basington?"

She freezes ever so slightly, and her fingers grip my hand tighter. If I wasn't already watching all her reactions, I'd have missed it.

"No, I moved here when I was eighteen." Her voice is soft, almost broken, and I hate it.

"You have family here?" I add.

She breaks another piece of the muffin off but plays with it in her fingers, her eyes staring into space. "Yeah."

"You don't want to talk about it?" I raise an eyebrow.

I scan her face, and she shakes her head gently from side to side.

"That's okay, beauty. You can tell me when you feel like it." I stroke my hand down her cheek tenderly, and the warmth seeping into my skin makes my cock ache painfully.

"Beauty?"

"Mmm?"

"I really need to empty my balls right now."

Tia bursts out laughing. "Oh my god, Cole. Talk about spoiling the moment!"

I grin at her triumphantly. "I know, but, Jesus, my cock is rubbing against my jeans and, beauty? It fucking hurts." I practically sulk as she shakes her head with laughter.

"You didn't wear boxers?"

I jolt at her words. "Fuck no. I got your address and came straight here."

Her spine straightens, and her face freezes. "Where did you get my address from?"

"Your manager at Envy gave it to me."

"What's his name?" she snaps back at me, clearly testing my answer.

"Reggie," I answer with a smile, remembering the information Lucas gave me about the club last week. He'd told me if I need anything while there, Reggie, the manager, would approve it. By "anything," he no doubt meant a lap dance or a quick fuck, but I don't have to pay women for that shit, not when I can get them to drop their panties just by smiling in their direction. Besides, I enjoy the chase. Not that there's normally much of that either.

Tia lets out a breath of air, and her shoulders slacken. She's clearly hiding shit with her reactions, but I look forward to finding out what.

A thought suddenly occurs to me, making my free hand ball into a fist. If she's hiding shit over some douche of an ex, I'd take great pleasure in fucking him up for even looking in her direction.

"Cole?"

Her words snap me out of my thoughts. "Huh?"

"What were you thinking about?"

"Do you have an ex-boyfriend?"

Her eyes widen, and her cheeks redden. *So damn cute.*

"N . . . No," she stammers. "I've never had a boyfriend."

My eyebrows knit together in confusion while I trail my eyes over my woman. "Never?"

She swallows. "No. I never wanted one."

Jesus, she's so damn perfect.

"Come 'ere." I gesture toward myself with a smirk as I open my legs for her to stand between them. The sway of her hips is masked beneath the baggy T-shirt, and my hands waste no time lifting it over her head, exposing her naked body to me.

I suck in a sharp breath at the sight before me. I've never seen anyone so beautiful in my entire life. Her plump tits are more than a handful—perfect—and her pebbled nipples are begging to be sucked.

She nibbles on her lip, waiting for me to respond, but I sit there feeling frozen to the spot, unsure what to do next, because this woman in front of me deserves so much more than me, but I sure as shit won't let her leave me. Not when I only just found her.

"Touch me," I tell her, hating the hint of vulnerability in my tone.

TIA

The vulnerable tone in Cole's voice makes me snap into action. I lead him to my room by my hand and push him to sit on my bed.

With each question I asked, I felt like I'd peeled a layer off his solid body, taking me further to his core, letting me see deep inside him and his wounds. He shared information with me I'm sure he's never shared before—openly admitting he doesn't date or do pillow talk—and that thought alone spurs me into action.

To make the big guy in front of me feel better, feel worthy.

Cole allows me to tug his T-shirt over his head. His golden skin is completely clear of tattoos. I ever so slowly trail my hand over his broad chest, over his solid pecs, and I finally still on his beating heart, which is currently hammering against my touch. His breathing has escalated.

"Tia?" he questions, breaking me out of my frozen state. His breath is a whisper over my cheek, sending a rush of arousal over my body. My nipples graze his chest, and he sucks in a sharp breath. "Beauty," he all but warns.

I straddle his thighs, and my wet pussy rests on his crotch as I begin to rock back and forth over him while clinging to his neck.

"Beauty, really need my cock inside you, otherwise, I'm going to come in my jeans. I'm that fucking close already."

I smile against Cole's head, then lean back, placing my hands onto his knees.

"Fucking, Jesus." His eyes growing hooded by the second, roam over my naked body. He pops open the buttons of his jeans. Sighing in relief, he allows his thick pierced cock to spring out, leaving behind a trail of sticky pre-cum. I lift myself up onto his waiting cock, and the stretch it causes heightens my already aroused state. The sting of pain with the mixture of pleasure urges me on.

Cole's eyes close as I lower myself down inch by pleasurable inch. "Fuck, beauty. Ride me, ride me, and let me watch those gorgeous tits bounce."

His words send a thrill through me as I rock myself back and forth on his lap. Easing his cock into me, his hands grip my hips tightly, and he bites the inside of his cheek, letting me know he's barely holding back.

"I love your cock filling me, Cole."

"Jesus. Fuck, I'm not going to last if you get all dirty on me."

"Do you want me to stop?" I stroke my hand down his chest all the way to where we're connected, and he follows the movement.

He shakes his head. "No, beauty, give it to me. Give me all your filthy mouth while you take mine." He sticks his tongue out, his piercing sparkling in the light.

I lean forward and suck it into my mouth, our kiss becoming ravenous as I bounce myself slowly on his cock. His piercing hits the perfect spot with each bounce, forcing a moan to vibrate in my throat and around his tongue.

Disconnecting the kiss, I lean forward and open the drawer beside the bed, taking out my purple vibrator.

Cole's eyes light up playfully. "Fuck yes! Put it in your mouth and suck it, beauty. Show me how good you take two cocks."

My pussy clenches at the thought of having more than one cock inside me, and my lips find the rubber on their own accord. Gently, I caress it with my tongue, moaning as I slide it inside.

One of his hands moves to my ass, gripping it tightly while the other helps me bounce up and down.

Cole pushes up into me, and I clench my pussy muscles around him.

"Fuck. That's good, beauty. Taking that cock in your mouth like my dirty whore."

I moan around the toy, and my clit throbs for contact.

Cole seems to realize this because he grinds up into me, causing the perfect amount of friction. Then, his thrusts become harder. It feels so damn good.

"Please," I beg around the toy. For what, I'm not sure.

"Gimme your tits, push them in my face, beauty. Keep sucking that cock. Keep sucking, beauty." He pants.

I press a breast to Cole's waiting lips. He tugs and

pulls on the nipple, sucking and swirling his piercing over the peak. The toy drops away from my mouth.

"Oh god, I'm going to come, Cole."

His thumb probes my ass, and I can't help but to push against him, allowing him access. I throw my head back as he rams into me.

"That's it, beauty, come on my cock. Let my cock fill this tight pussy hole full of cum. Let my thumb fuck that little ass."

He sucks to the point of pain on my nipple, and a wave of euphoria takes over me. "Yessss."

"Fuck. Fuck, beauty." His cock swells inside me, and his cum floods my pussy, forcing his movements to become labored before he drops his head against the pillow. My tits practically smother his face.

I hold his head there as he gently sucks the flesh of my tit, marking it and making his cock twitch in response.

"You're mine, beauty," he mumbles, and his words don't scare me like I'd always suspected they would. The last time I was told this, I gave not only my body away but my heart too. Only to be betrayed in the worst kind of way.

I hold him closer, enjoying the warmth of him against me and believing every word he tells me.

"When you pull off of me, I want you to coat your tits in my cum."

I pull back from him to search his face, looking for any sign of insincerity. I smile back at his transfixed eyes. As I ease off his cock, I do as instructed and move my hand directly to my pussy. Cupping the cum dripping from me, I bring it to my tits and rub it over them while I watch him stroke his cock up and down. Still straddling his lap, I tweak my nipples with his essence and watch him lose control.

"Fuck. I'm going to cover you in my cum, beauty. Tell me you want it."

My mouth parts in wonder at Cole's words. I move my finger over my engorged clit and rub it aggressively, already feeling the telltale sign of another orgasm. "Please. Cover me in your cum, Cole," I beg.

"Fuck yes." Cole's lips part as his cum hits my stomach, tits, and chest. With my free hand, I rub it in, letting his mark of ownership seep inside me, deep inside me.

We pant in unison.

"I love you covered in my cum, beauty."

I giggle at his words. "I gathered. Now I need to shower again."

Cole's hands tighten on my hips. "Don't. I don't want you to shower, I want you to stay like that."

My eyebrows rise. "You're serious?"

"Damn fucking right I am. When you leave this apartment, I want you covered in me."

I watch Cole's face for a sign of playfulness, but both the seriousness on his face and the tone of his voice lets me know he's absolutely serious.

"Is this . . . is this a kink of yours?"

His eyebrows knit together. "Not that I'm aware of. Another first for me, I guess." He shrugs.

I can't help but like the idea that he's never done this to anyone else, only me.

He brushes a few locks of hair from my face. "I told you that you're special, beauty."

I nod at his words and swallow thickly. "You're special too, Cole. I can feel it."

Cole's face breaks out into a huge smile. "You can, huh? You're mine, Tia." His eyes hold me hostage, forcing me to agree. I nibble my lip and give him a small nod.

COLE

I've been in Basington over two weeks now, and I've loved being with Tia every night. We've spent every hour she doesn't work together, and I can't imagine what my life would be like without her in it. My chest hurts at the thought, the feeling completely alien to me.

But Lucas is getting antsy with the constant calls. He's desperate for me to return home, and if I were being honest with myself, my business here is done.

The gym he sent me to is now being signed over to us, and Lucas is arranging for a new manager to take over. I was tempted to take control myself, therefore being able to stay here with Tia, but truth be told, I'm missing Lucas. I'm missing both of my brothers. As much as I know I'm falling for Tia, I also love them. They're family, and I want her to be family too.

I've researched her college course, and it's online based, so in reality, she can do it anywhere and submit her work at the college local to us.

She doesn't need to work because I earn enough

money for the both of us, but if she has issue with that, I can deal with that too. I just want her, in whatever capacity.

She's it for me.

"You look deep in thought. Is everything okay?" Tia places down her burger and gives me her full attention. Her blue eyes stun me each time I stare into them. When she's aroused, they go a deeper shade, yet when she's sad, they appear to lighten. They're unique.

"Everything's fine, beauty. I'm just thinking about home, that's all."

Her face falls. "Oh."

She quickly tries to hide the look of disappointment and panic, but I don't miss it, and I can't help but be hopeful that she needs me in her life as much as I need her.

"Do you need to leave soon?"

I shake my head and take another sip of my soda. "We're good just yet." I lie to her to subside my own feelings, not daring to risk losing her so soon into starting a relationship with her.

We've spent every night together, and when she has lunch hour at the diner—like today—I join her. Then, I spend my evenings growling at every asshole who dares look in her direction when she works at the club. She moaned that I was affecting her tips, so now I stuff a few hundred dollars extra in the jar each night to cover any losses.

I decide to change the subject, hiding my concerns in denial. "What time do you get off?"

"Five." She picks at the bun, clearly just as affected with the conversation as me.

"You fancy a walk in the park when you finish? You're not working tonight, right?"

Tia smiles at me, and my heart seems to swell at her happiness. "I'm off tonight, and that sounds amazing. Thank you." She bends forward and pecks my lips, but I take a hold of her chin and gift my girl with my pierced tongue, deepening the kiss until her moans of pleasure vibrate against me.

CHAPTER

FIVE

Tia

We've spent all evening wandering around the town of Basington. I showed Cole the bar I used to work at, we picked up a few groceries, and looked around a few stores. The area in which I live in is okay, but nowhere near as nice as the next town over, Chester.

Properties sell for millions of dollars in Chester. Children go to elite private schools, and stores are known boutiques. It's the perfect family town for young professional families, somewhere I'll never be able to afford nor fit in.

We're sitting in the park with sandwiches, watching the kids play on the nearby playground in a comfortable silence. Cole watches the children chasing one another with a smile playing on his lips, and my heart does a little flutter at the softness in his expression, giving me the courage to do something I've never done before.

"I have a daughter."

I can feel Cole's eyes snap to mine, but I stare ahead,

unprepared to witness the disappointment in his expression. Something inside me tells me to be open with him, that I can trust him, and maybe, just maybe, he can help me somehow.

And if we're going to be in some sort of relationship, I need him to know. I need him to know about her.

"Her name's Harper, and she's four years old."

"Does she live with her dad?" Cole waits expectantly for me to continue.

My heart thumps in my ears, my chest heaving.

I stare out at the children playing, imagining Harper among them. "No." I clear my throat. "She has a placement with a couple."

"Placement?" I flinch at Cole's tone. He's mad. I'm not surprised, I know I'm a bad mother, one who could barely feed her baby.

"Like foster care?" His words are sharp, cutting deep in my heart at the accusation behind them. He knows firsthand children don't go into care for no reason. No, they go there because there's no other choice. Their parents let them down and are incapable of caring for them. My heart constricts at the thought.

My eyes fill with tears. "She deserves better," I whisper the words, but he picks up on them anyway.

"Damn fucking right she deserves better. What kind of mother are you?" He spits the words like venom, and they hurt just like they were meant to.

They cut deep, forcing me to close my eyes at the searing pain I feel when my chest closes up, hearing him utter the words I've heard multiple times. Yet, I still cling on to the hope that one day—*one day*—I might be good enough for her.

His rage radiates from him; the heat of his temper forces me to shuffle away slightly. My body is shutting down, and I pull my knees up to my chest and cling to them for comfort.

He moves closer to me, his mouth close to my ear. "Do you know what happens to kids in care? Do you know what some poor kids go through?" he hisses out venomously.

My spine bolts straight with anger, and I jump to my feet. He follows suit, and the anger building inside me makes me snap as I spin to face him. "How dare you? How dare you fucking judge me? You know nothing about me, Cole. Nothing. And here I was thinking we had some sort of connection, that I could trust you!" I poke my finger into his chest, forcing him to take a step back in shock at my reaction. Well, screw him and his words.

My chest heaves, and tears streak down my face as I point toward my chest. "I know what it feels like. I know what some sick bastards are capable of, and without a shadow of a doubt, I would do every fucking thing in my power to stop that, so don't you dare tell me I don't know what happens in care. Don't you fucking dare!"

COLE

Tia's angry face morphs into heartbreak the moment I utter the words, "Do you know what happens to kids in care? Do you know what some kids go through?"

I couldn't help the vitriol that spewed from me. Knowing what my brothers have been through, knowing the traumas that shaped them into the vulnerable, angry, detached people they are today made me lash out and say hurtful, hate-filled shit to her.

I felt that I had to defend them in some way, make her somehow realize the consequences of such decisions as putting your child in care. And for what? Because she doesn't have a good job? Because some dick knocked her up and didn't stick around?

No, that's inexcusable. There is never a reason for your child to be in care. Not in my opinion, at least.

But after witnessing the heartbreak on her face and watching her expression crumble in front of my very eyes, I knew that decision wasn't taken lightly. Shit, I knew she never had any other choice, and when her spine went as straight as steel and she uttered those words to me, I knew.

"I know what it feels like. I know what some sick bastards are capable of, and without a shadow of a doubt, I would do every fucking thing in my power to stop that, so don't you dare tell me I don't know what happens in care. Don't you fucking dare!"

I knew, without a shadow of a doubt, my girl's been through hell—maybe even still going through hell—and I just accused her of being a bad mother. The worst kind of mother.

My shoulders slacken, and I take a step toward her, but she steps back, taking a chunk of my heart with her.

"Tia . . . I . . ."

She shakes her head vigorously, her lip trembling. "I don't want to hear it, Cole. I don't want to hear anything you have to say to me."

My heart races in panic, and my hands tremble at the thought of me not only hurting her, destroying her soul, but her leaving here without me.

She turns her back and begins to walk away, but I'll be damned if she leaves me like this, leaves *us* like this.

I rush toward her and spin her to face me, bending slightly to rest my forehead against hers. I swallow thickly, her eyes refusing to meet mine.

"Beauty. Fuck." I scrub a hand over my head. "I'm sorry. Please. Please, look at me."

Slowly, her eyes rise, hurt seeping through them, causing my breath to stutter. Tears streak her beautiful face, and I hate myself for causing them. I vow, here and fucking now, to never make my girl cry again. Never.

"I'm sorry." I take a hold of her hand and place it over my beating heart, hoping the thundering in my chest will dissipate at her gentle touch, hoping she can see and feel the truth from inside me. "I'm sorry," I repeat once again.

I audibly exhale when her tense shoulders drop, and she gives me a small nod, then turns her head away from me. I know I've fucked up. Jesus, do I know it.

But I follow her back toward her apartment like a lost puppy, desperate for her not to cut me off completely.

Tia passes me a bottle of water from the refrigerator, then sits in the chair opposite me—the one next to the table and not beside me on the couch. That action alone hurts.

I feel like a pussy, but I need her to want me like I desperately want her. Instead, she's choosing to put distance between us, and it feels like she's on the other side of the world right now.

Tia dips her head and stares at her bare feet. "I had Harper when I was sixteen."

I suck in a breath—because, Jesus, that's young.

Watching her closely, she sounds almost robotic as she speaks, staring at the carpet instead of toward me, as though she's completely detaching herself.

"I'd been in care my whole life, Cole." Her distraught eyes meet mine, and I want to reach out and hold her, stroke her hair, and tell her how sorry I am.

I move to stand, but she shakes her head and holds

her hand up to stop me. So, my sorry ass lands back on the couch.

"I never intended on getting pregnant." She shakes her head. "I'm not stupid, Cole." She looks at me pointedly. "I had dreams, big dreams." Her tear-filled eyes look up toward the ceiling as she tries to fight her emotions.

"I was in love with a boy older than me." My pulse races when she mentions some jumped-up punk, and I want to pummel him for leaving her in that mess. "He wasn't my baby's father." My breath stutters as I wait for her to elaborate.

Her body visibly shakes, and her chin wobbles. I clench my fists to stop me from reaching out, but I know she needs to do this alone. Like she always has.

"What I'm about to tell you—" She swallows harshly. "You can never tell anyone else. Swear it."

I stare at her in shock. She's trusting me, after how I treated her. Accused her of such shit. She's trusting me.

"Please," she vulnerably tacks on at the end, causing my heart to dip at her words.

I know what she says next is going to be bad. I can see it as clear as day. It's painted on her face, it's locked up tight inside her, screaming to get out, desperate to trust someone but not knowing who.

I raise my head and straighten my shoulders; I'll be that for her. I'll be the man she needs, the one she confides in, the one to protect her at all costs.

"I'm here for you, beauty." I stare into her eyes with a confidence that emanates from me. Her shoulders relax, and she licks her lips nervously.

"I . . . I . . ." She wrings her hands together and takes a deep breath. "I was forced. While I was in care."

I suck in a sharp breath, my body tightening to the point of pain. My jaw locks, and my eyes flare with rage—an indescribable rage. I need to kill someone, make them fucking pay for hurting her.

My eyes meet hers, and my heart shatters.

"They took her from me. They said I wasn't a suitable mother, that my mental health wasn't stable enough."

My mind goes fucking wild. What the fuck? Not stable enough? A fucking child was raped while in care, and they tear her baby from her?

"Where is she now?" I snipe the words out and instantly regret them when she jolts. I sigh and get up from the couch, not giving her the choice but to let her know I'm here for her.

For both of them.

I kneel at her feet so we're face-to-face, me and my beauty. Gently, I tuck the tear-drenched locks from her face behind her ear. "Where is she, beauty?"

"She's been with a couple in care since she was six months old." Her chest begins to rise and fall rapidly. "They said they can offer her a better life without me."

Anger boils inside me. They want to shut her out? Her own mother?

"They have money, Cole. They want to adopt her."

My eyes flare at her words.

"That's not what I want." Tia shakes her head from side to side. "I want my baby. She's mine, and they won't give her back!" She yells the last part before she drops her head onto my shoulder and cries uncontrollably into my neck. My arms band around her, holding her tightly.

There's no fucking way I'll let them take her away from Tia. No fucking way.

"It's okay, beauty. I got you. Shhh, please don't cry." I hate it, hate hearing her sobs, her pain.

I scoop her off the chair and into my arms, carrying her toward her bedroom, dropping kisses onto her head as she sobs deep into my neck.

"Hush, beauty. I got you."

—▪—

T ia
I spent the night crying into Cole's chest as he gently soothed me like a child. I can't remember the last time that happened, a man being there for me. That's a lie, I do remember. Yet he destroyed me.

I suck in a breath at the pain that memory still causes.

Thalia

Aged Sixteen

Jace strokes his hand up and down my spine tenderly while I rest on his naked chest. "Did I hurt you?"

"No."

"I'm going to miss you." He takes a hold of my chin gently. "You need to be strong, Thalia. As soon as I'm settled in college, I can pick you up for weekends. Okay?"

I nod gingerly, darting my eyes away, unsure of what he's promising.

"Look at me, Thalia."

Tears fill my eyes.

"Baby, listen to me. I know what you're thinking. I know you think as soon as I leave here, I'm going to forget about you."

How does he do this? How does he know my fears so well?

"I'm not. I could never forget you, baby, never. You hear me?"

I nibble at my lip nervously as I contemplate my next words, not wanting to anger nor disappoint him. I swirl my finger over his chest, watching as goose bumps break out over his skin. "What about . . ."

"Sex?" His nostrils flare, but I nod anyway. It's a legitimate worry of mine; he's a gorgeous seventeen-year-old guy who could easily pass for older. Plus, Jace has such a way with numbers that he's been able to skip two years of school and achieve an all-expenses-paid scholarship to the top university in Hanover: the University of New Hampshire. So, yeah, I'm worried someone is going to try and snag my guy, no matter how many times he promises me otherwise.

"I told you, Thalia. You. Are. It. For. Me. I'll wait." His eyes bore into mine, the truth evident in his words, mirrored on his expression.

Gently, Jace's lips meet mine in an all-consuming kiss that sends a tsunami of emotions flooding through me. A kiss of truth, determination, love. A kiss that tells me a thousand things without uttering a single word.

I'm his, he's mine, and we'll wait for one another. Because love is worth waiting for, and Jace Matthews loves me with every fiber of his being, he loves me with everything he has, everything he wants, and everything he's going to become.

He pulls back from me and stares into my eyes. "One day,

you'll be Thalia Matthews, and until then, I'd wait a lifetime for you."

I wish I knew then what I know now: How on that very morning of him leaving me it would be the last time I'd ever see him again. How all the whispered promises would be broken, shattered to a million pieces, destroyed by not only his actions but those he left me with.

I know now that when he walked out that door with trepidation in his eyes, he left knowing the trauma I was going to face time and time again, and the words of love and promises he made to me when he fucked me into the mattress with his condom-covered dick was just another of the multiple lies he told me.

I know that for years I've refused to let anyone get close to me with fear of not being able to trust in anyone—to confide in them—was all due to the barriers I created because of him. I also know that without the hurt of that boy I thought I loved, I'd have never been on the path that I'm on right now.

I'd never have found the love, comfort, and protectiveness I find when I stare into the eyes of Cole Maguire.

Jace Matthews may have shattered my heart, but Cole Maguire has rebuilt it.

COLE

I let Tia sleep through the evening and into the night, holding her close to me. I alternated from having my arms banded tightly around her to slowly stroking her hair when her ragged breaths turned to whimpers.

She stirred in the night, rambling incoherent words, and it was obvious her sharing her story with me had brought back her trauma.

I want to kill the sick bastard who touched her, gut him slowly. And I will. But first, I need to reassure her that I'm here for her no matter what, her and her little girl, because I'll be damned if I let some rich fucks from Chester bring up her daughter. Not when she has a loving home here with us.

"I can hear you thinking." Her soft voice trickles over my skin, and I squeeze her tighter.

"I'm going to help you get Harper back where she belongs."

Tia's head snaps up toward mine, her mouth open in shock. "How?"

"I have ways."

I shrug a shoulder, and Tia darts up, kneeling to stare down at me. "No, Cole. I can't do anything to risk them taking her from me."

I glide my hand up her thigh and lace our fingers together. "Beauty, they already took her."

She shakes her head. "More. They can force the adoption through, they told me. Warned me they'd do it." Her chest rises, panic visible on her face.

"Tell me, who warned you?"

"The Lancasters, her foster parents. They want to adopt her, but I won't sign the papers. They have a lawyer, Cole. A freaking lawyer." She jumps to her feet and starts pacing. "Look at me . . ." Her words are broken, full of torment.

I stare my girl up and down, looking at her. I see her.

"I see you, beauty."

She chokes on a sarcastic laugh. "I'm a twenty-one-year-old student in a one-bedroom apartment who is juggling two jobs just to try and get more than the two hours a month with my lawyer so I can try and fight this. What the hell do I have to offer her, Cole?"

Anger boils inside me. She's been fighting this alone for too long, far too fucking long, and I refuse to let her fight it alone any longer. "We're getting her back." I stand with a steel determination. "Let me call my brother; he'll know what to do."

Her eyes bug out. "What? No. I . . ." Tia begins to shake, panic taking over her small body. I step toward her and pull her into me. "I don't want anyone to know."

Shame drips from her words, and I hate it. She has nothing to be ashamed of. Absolutely nothing.

I stroke over her hair and kiss her head. "I know, beauty. But this, please trust me." Pulling back, our eyes fix on one another's.

"Can you . . . can you ask him not to dig too deep? Just up to when I had Harper?"

I jolt at her words. Does she not trust me? What the fuck? Is she hiding some shit from me?

As if hearing my thoughts, she goes on to explain, "I haven't dealt with my past, Cole, and I don't want to. Please." The desperation for me to agree seeps into her eyes, and I know I have to lie to her, because I know, without a shadow of a doubt, I'll make whoever hurt my girl pay.

CHAPTER
SEVEN

Lucas

My phone vibrates across my desk, and I sigh heavily, knowing Cole is going to give me more excuses as to why he can't come home yet.

This girl he's fixated on must have one hell of a magnetic pussy because his pierced cock is well and truly attached.

For the first time in his womanizing life, he's fucking one woman. Rage laughed when I told him Cole refused to come home because the dipshit claims to be in love. How the fuck he thinks he can be in love is beyond me. I guess I always assumed my brothers were immune to it, much like me.

Rage has a deep-seated hate toward the only girl he ever claimed to feel anything for. She broke his heart and kicked his ass to the curb a long time ago, and since that day, we gave him the nickname "Rage" based purely on his spiraling, uncontrollable anger at the mere thought of the girl.

I press the speaker button on my phone. "Are you coming home?" I snap into the empty room, causing an echo to bounce off the walls.

My muscles bunch in annoyance at his lack of concern about me or his brother. No, he fucks off over two hours away to Shitsville with no thought as to how his absence has impacted the business. Or us.

"I need help, man." His voice is so low—almost a whisper—that it sets the hairs at the back of my neck on edge.

I sit forward in my office chair. "What's wrong? Are you okay?" My body shakes at the thought of him not being close and in danger.

"I'm fine. Shit, it's not me."

My shoulders sag. My concern for him breezed over as usual. It's not him, so it must be her, of course. The girl who's holding him back, stopping him from coming home to his family, where he belongs.

The anguish in Cole's voice makes me put my feelings aside, because no matter what, I'll always be here for him, like he's always here for me.

"What do you need?"

"Tia. She's been through some shit, man. Real shit. Trauma."

My pulse accelerates at the sound of his voice, the word he uses to describe her problems. I know he wouldn't use that word without good cause, and that alone escalates my need to help him and, indirectly, her too.

"What kind of . . .?" I can't say the word, the one they used so regularly to describe my absent behavior.

70

Emotion, a pain clawing at my chest, swells inside me, eager to get out.

Cole senses my inner struggle, as always, and he grounds me. "She has a daughter."

My body jolts at this new information. "A daughter?"

"Yeah, but they took her away . . ."

Before he can utter another word, my own tumble from my mouth like poison. "Well, what the fuck did she do to her?"

"Do. Not. Fucking. Accuse. Her. Of. Shit, Lucas. I won't stand for it! You hear me?"

My hands shake at the venom behind his words, my body frozen in shock. Never before has Cole sided with anyone, anyone but me. I don't know whether to be pissed or filled with pride. Clearly, she means something to him. My heart hammers in my chest. Would he pick her over me?

"Are you listening, Lucas?"

I swallow past the lump of insecurity. "Yeah."

"I need this to be between me and you."

"Why?"

"Because I trust you, man."

My heart hammers against my chest. He came to me with this because he trusts me. "Of course." Even though he can't see me, I nod—like an idiot.

"Okay, so she had her while in care." Straight away, I feel for the girl because being in care is bad enough in the first place, but having a kid while there? I can understand where Cole's need to protect her is coming from.

"Some sick fuck knocked her up."

And just like that, my stomach flips, my body shakes,

and I barely make it over to the trash can in time to empty the meager contents of my stomach up.

The room is filled with a deafening silence as I swipe my hand across my mouth.

"Lucas, are you okay?"

My body trembles uncontrollably. "Yes." It's a lie. He knows it. I know it. I'm not okay. I won't ever be okay.

"I'm sorry, man, I know how hard this shit is for you."

I pull out my pen knife, the one that helps. The wooden handle is smooth to the touch. I stroke it, calming from the security of having it in my hand. I flick the blade back and forth, back and forth.

Turning to face the desk, I stare at the phone.

"Do you think you can help?" His plea hangs heavily in the room. He knows how I feel about delving into such topics. "I just . . . I don't know what to do. It's more the legal side of things. They're trying to force her to give her little girl up for adoption, Lucas. She doesn't want that; she wants to be a mom."

My heart aches for the girl, for Cole too. His need to protect her and do the right thing bleeds from him. He's always the good guy, the one who wants to make things right when the world we live in is so wrong.

"Of course I'll help. But . . ." My words hang in the air, thick with insecurity—a vulnerability—that I hate. "Can you come home?" I drop back down into my leather chair, my eyes locked on the phone, waiting for a response. Desperation oozes from me. I stroke the soft wood and wait.

"Yeah, I figured I'd bring Tia with me?" It's a question, not a statement, and he's awaiting my approval.

"Of course. I want to meet the girl you claim to love," I joke with him, trying to disguise the excitement that knowing he's coming home brings me. If it means I have to play nice and like the girl, I will. I can. For him.

"I don't claim, Lucas. I know," he bites back, but with a playfulness in his tone.

I smile at the phone with a newfound confidence. "Okay. Bring her back, and I'll start looking into things. We'll get her daughter back."

"Oh, Lucas . . ." He pauses and makes a ruffling noise. I close my eyes and imagine him brushing a hand over his short, cropped hair, hair I long to touch. "She asked for me not to dig back too far in her life." Cole sighs, as though he's uncomfortable with his own words, battling an inner demon. He doesn't want to delve deeper into her past, he wants to do the honorable thing, but he also wants to know what she wants to stay hidden, no doubt to protect her.

"I'll let you know if there's anything you need to be aware of," I conclude for him, taking the decision from his hands. "Monday, bring her Monday," I quickly spit out, almost forgetting the importance behind the date.

He exhales loudly in relief, and I almost want to chuckle at the thought of how much Cole wears his heart and expressions on his sleeve.

"Thanks, man. I'll see you soon, brother."

"Yeah." I end the call, never liking to say goodbye.

My body sags with the knowledge I hold in my hands, the heavy weight of a secret I've been keeping for a while now. I glance toward the file spread out on my desk. Her face smiles back at me, blue eyes shining so bright they make my pulse race. Her slim yet shapely body makes my cock thicken in my pants, and the thought of my brother fucking her causes pre-cum to drip from the tip.

I trace my finger over her face and down her body. What secrets does she have hidden?

Why is there no mention of a daughter in her file?

What life has she led before she became Tia Jones, living in the care of the state?

What I do know is I won't stop until I uncover the truth behind her and her daughter. I'll bring them here for Cole and make us the perfect family.

A loud thud breaks my train of thought.

"Lucas, are you in there?"

"Yeah, wait a sec." I scoop the file up and open the drawer with my key, dumping it inside and locking it away where it belongs.

For now.

Then, I press the button beneath my desk that unlocks my door.

Rage storms into the room like a goddamn hurricane, and I sigh, leaning back into my chair in annoyance.

"You have your cock out or something?"

My eyes meet his raging ones in confusion. "Huh?"

"The door." He points toward the door. "You locked it again."

"Oh. No."

Rage smirks, as though he knows something I don't.

"Cole is coming home. He's bringing the girl with him."

Rage's eyes bug out. "He's serious about her?"

I shrug nonchalantly. "He's in love."

Rage scoffs. "Right." He rolls his eyes mockingly. "About fucking time he came home!" He chooses to completely ignore the fact that Cole is bringing home his girlfriend.

"He gets back Monday," I add.

Rage muses on my words. "Mmm, I leave Sunday. Shit, I was hoping to catch up with him. I'm not going to be here for two weeks." He sighs heavily, obviously dejected with Cole's absence.

I nod in agreement, lowering my eyes from his face.

"Well, at least I don't have to watch him play happy fucking families with her." He snipes the words out coldly.

Rage hates any form of emotion toward a female. He "fucks them, then chucks them" as he once said. He finds them undeserving. According to him, all females are liars. His ex really did a number on him to the point he sees them all the same.

I decide to withhold the information that we have on her daughter joining us soon too. Knowing this will probably tip him over the fucking edge.

"A fucking female around here. Fan-fucking-tastic." He stews as he turns on his heel and saunters back down the corridor.

"You ordering pizza, or am I?!" he shouts as he walks away. Because we're both shit when Cole isn't here to organize us.

"You!" I bellow back.

"Prick!"

If only he knew how true that was.

My eyes involuntarily latch on to the locked drawer.

Where secrets are hidden, set to destroy us all.

But maybe, just maybe, they can fix us all too.

EIGHT

━━◆━━

C ole

Tia's leg bounces uncontrollably as we drive toward the Lancasters' mansion in Chester.

My mind wanders. Is she like this every time she has her visitation with her daughter?

"So, you get to see her once a month?" I glance toward her as she stares out of the window.

"Yes. It started out as more, but they're slowly trying to shove me out of the picture. Each time they get granted more, I struggle to pay the bills to fight it."

I nod in understanding as my eyes take in the rows of mansions along the estate. "How long do you get her for?"

"Ten until four." Tia stares out of the window. Her face looks defeated and pained, as though she's battling inner thoughts.

"I have money, Tia. Besides, all this doesn't mean shit." I wave my hand out at the perfectly manicured lawns. "What matters is you're her mom, beauty. You love her more than anyone else on this goddamn earth. That's what matters."

She turns her head to face me, and a sad smile graces her lips. Her face is full of sadness but a tinge of hope also sparks in her eyes.

I take her hand in mine, lacing our fingers together before bringing them to my mouth and gently kissing them.

"It's this one here." Tia points toward the imposing Victorian-looking mansion with the gates already opened. It shouldn't piss me off, but it does. Where is the security?

A tremble vibrates through Tia, and I choose to ignore it. Instead, anger builds inside me at how disgusting this whole setup is. She seems terrified at the thoughts of the visitation, which is absurd.

I pull the car up outside of the house. It's dated but well kept. It's something I imagine has been in a family for generations, and I can't help but think that they need to get their own family instead of trying to steal Tia's. Mine.

"Cole, can you not say anything to them?" Concern mars her face. My eyes narrow in confusion, forcing her to elaborate. "If they say anything you don't like, please don't retaliate. Promise me." Her hand tightens on mine, and her eyes implore me to agree.

The look of sheer despair on her face makes my heart race. The thought of something upsetting them leaves her with nothing more than what can be described as terror for her, and I want to kill them for it.

I find myself agreeing with her just to make her feel comfortable. "Sure."

Her shoulders relax slightly before she licks her lips, takes a deep breath, and steels herself. With shaky hands, she opens the door.

Anger bubbles inside me. The gravity of the situation we're about to walk into is unmistakable, but I'll do what she asks. I'll support her.

For now, I'll play nice, while behind the scenes, Lucas is working toward getting Harper back where she belongs: with her mom.

TIA

My hands shake as I press the doorbell. Cole's presence behind me is a comfort I'm not used to, but one I welcome wholeheartedly.

It's something I've never had before, someone to support me—not in a long time anyway, and he only turned out to be someone else who let me down eventually, feeding me to the wolves and walking away.

I shake the thoughts of him away and concentrate on the here and now.

The clicking of Mrs. Lancaster's heels gets closer as she approaches the solid wood door, and sickness gathers in my stomach. With as much money as they have, they decided to keep the Victorian features of the property. With it comes the ability to hear through the single paned windows and doors. Many a time I have caught the end of conversations about me. About Harper.

"It's okay, beauty. I'm here." Cole's hand glides over my sweater and sits low on my back. I melt into him. The warmth of his hand seeps through the material and onto my skin, creating a newly found inner strength.

The door opens, and as always, my heart races at the feeling of being intimidated, feeling looked down on and worthless, when Mrs. Lancaster glares down her nose at me.

Her appearance is always professional looking: her neck scarf is tight around her throat, her white blouse is tucked into her black pencil skirt, and she has black heels and stockings. Her hair is always tied tightly up in a bun, and her makeup is impeccable, unlike my chipped black nail varnish I'm currently nibbling on.

As always, she slowly trails her eyes from the bottom of my combat boots up my jeans, slowly up my sweater—the one I purposely put on to cover my chest when she said I was advertising myself in a sexual manner around Harper. My leather jacket has been hand washed, and my normally light makeup is absent so I don't mislead Harper down a path of wrongdoings. Then, her cruel eyes latch on to mine.

They hold me hostage, making my heart race faster and causing my body to tremble. I feel like she's looking into my soul, like she's seeing all the disgusting, dirty things about me, and this only makes her despise me all the more.

A throat behind me clears and I jolt, forgetting for a moment that Cole is here too. For me.

Mrs. Lancaster's eyes widen, as though she's only just making the same realization.

"You'd best come in. It appears we need to talk, Tia."

She raises an eyebrow on a sneer before turning and walking inside.

I follow behind her, my eyes searching the enormous entrance for a sign of Harper, anything to show me that my little girl lives here, that she's happy.

Cole's strong presence behind me gives me a confidence I don't normally feel. It gives me hope.

Stepping into the kitchen, Mrs. Lancaster leans against the countertop. "Who is he?"

She doesn't so much as look in Cole's direction. I can feel him straighten beside me, and I beg for him not to react, not to make a scene, not to give her ammunition to keep Harper away from me.

My heart races in a panic when Cole steps aside. He holds out his hand. "I'm Cole Maguire. Nice to meet you, Mrs. Lancaster."

My mouth drops open in shock before I quickly mask it.

Mrs. Lancaster glares at Cole's outstretched hand as though it's poisonous before finally relenting and reluctantly shaking it. She quickly pulls away and picks up a hand towel, wiping away Cole's touch. The action makes me squirm uncomfortably, and I don't miss the noise of Cole's shocked choke.

"So, who are you, and what are you doing here?" Her eyes narrow on him, and disgust oozes from her eyes, the glare in them a mixture of both malice and disgust.

I take a glance at Cole. He dressed up for today, wearing gray slacks, brown dress shoes, and a white shirt that's tight over his muscular shoulders. He looks professional and hot; the thought makes me proud that he's my man. As if hearing my thoughts, he takes a sidestep toward me and entwines our fingers.

"I'm Tia's boyfriend, and I'm here to meet *her* daughter." I bristle with nervousness at his emphasis.

Mrs. Lancaster doesn't miss the dig either. Her eyes blacken and her nostrils flare. Her fingers grip the countertop until her knuckles are white.

"As you know, Tia, any change in circumstances needs to be given in writing. You cannot simply show up here and expect us to be okay with this." She waves her hand toward Cole but refuses to acknowledge him.

I release a tremble of panic. She's not going to let me see her.

Cole's shoulders expand. "As you know, Mrs. Lancaster, as per your legal documentation, you cannot refuse Tia access to her daughter without your legal representative being informed."

Oh shit, what's he doing?

"I contacted your lawyer this morning and gave proof of my clean record as well as my personal and business details. He's well aware I'm a good, clean influence to have around Tia and Harper, therefore, there's really no issue here today." I watch with bated breath at their standoff, the air thick with venom. "Of course, if you'd like to break the contract, my own legal team is on standby," Cole adds.

My eyes widen in shock.

Mrs. Lancaster takes her time to process her thoughts, watching Cole with a calculated scrutiny before the veins in her neck finally relax. She leans over the counter and picks up the bell, giving it a shake.

The ringing of the bell makes me wince. I hate it.

I hate it for so many reasons, but first and foremost, I hate it because the ringing of the bell is to instruct my daughter's nanny to bring her to me like cattle being called for food.

I hear her before I see her. The sheer delight in her voice makes my heart hammer against my chest.

Without thinking, I release Cole's hand and move toward the corridor to embrace my little girl.

C ole

I hate the bitch. She tries staring me down as Tia virtually runs toward her little girl.

The calculated look in her eyes fires vitriol in my direction, and I smirk at her in response.

"You don't look like a businessman." She raises a perfectly manicured eyebrow, and I'm both shocked and impressed that damn thing actually moves; it looks like her face has been lasered to make her appear younger. My eyes rake over her body in contempt, my lip curling for added effect.

How the fuck she can think she's better than us is beyond me. She's a Grade-A bitch with a stick so far up her ass, I'm surprised she isn't growing leaves out of her fake lips.

Clearly, she's older than she's portraying—the lines on her neck are a dead giveaway—although she's tried to hide them with the scarf she's wielding.

I want to use it to throttle the life out of her, and I will, but for now, I need to bide my time.

"You don't look like someone young enough to want a family. How can I put this politely . . ." I pause for effect. "Oh, I can't. You look old enough to be Harper's grandma. What's all that about? Too dried up to have kids of your own?"

The hag sucks in a sharp breath. "How dare you!" she hisses in my direction.

"Oh, I dare. And I dare to go so much further . . ." I smile at her manically. "If you try and keep Harper from my girl one more time, you'll see how far I dare to go."

The atmosphere between us is deadly, my words hanging thickly in the air. Her pompous chin raises as though unperturbed. But I know better; I see her flushed cheeks and hear her heart racing below that hideous blouse.

"Cole, I'd like you to meet Harper." Her soft voice washes over me from behind, and when I turn to face Tia, I see the hope in her eyes, a light of happiness shining through, begging to not be extinguished.

A shuffle behind her draws me to my knees so I'm level with the little girl hiding behind Tia's legs.

I soften my deep voice so not to scare her. "Hey there, Harper. It's good to meet you."

She steps out from behind Tia. Her blue eyes meet mine, and I'm jolted with an awareness of familiarity. She's Tia's double just in a smaller form, and right then and there, I instantly love her.

"Hi."

"I heard that you like the park. Is that true?"

Harper nods her head.

"Is it okay if I tag along? I'm real good at pushing swings."

Harper lets out an adorable giggle. "Can we have ice cream?" Her eyes light up in expectation.

"No," her sharp voice snaps from behind. "I've told you before, Harper. Ballet dancers don't eat ice cream. It makes them gain weight. You want to be a ballet dancer, don't you?"

Harper nods.

"Words, Harper. Use your words," the bitch snaps from behind, and I swear to God, it takes everything in me not to snap her neck. My hands tighten, balling into fists. Tia places a reassuring hand on Harper's shoulder, and, possibly without realizing, she draws her closer toward her. Any doubt anyone could have about Tia's intentions toward Harper would be extinguished within just this short length of time seeing them together.

"Y-Yes, ma'am." Harper's words come out shakily, making my teeth grit. No child should react the way Harper reacts to her.

"Okay, no ice cream," I say the words while still kneeling, but a smile plays on my lips, and I give Harper a little wink, causing her to grin back at me knowingly.

TIA

As soon as the car door closes, I relax. Harper is strapped in the car seat I normally carry from taxi to house and back again.

"Mommy, did you bring me a change of clothes?" her soft voice whispers through the car.

"Yes, peanut, don't worry."

Cole glances my way in question, so I go on to explain, "The Lancasters don't like her to return dirty."

His eyebrows furrow in confusion. "She's a kid."

"Right." A smile tugs at my lips. The fact that he agrees with me and understands how absurd that is makes me exhale in relief.

"I change her in the restrooms so we can play, then I change her back before taking her back there."

I can't bring myself to say *Take her home* because that isn't her home. Her home is with me, wherever I am. That's her home.

Cole pulls into the parking lot, and Harper unbuckles

her belt. "Come on, Cole, I need to show you the slides here."

She pushes open the car door before I can think to stop her, always so excitable and eager. Cole chuckles beside me and shakes his head before leaping out of the car and chasing after her.

I grab the bag containing her change of clothes and head out after them.

I watch as Cole pushes Harper higher, and her squeal of delight fills the playground. I take her in again. The pink hoodie she wears has a glitter rainbow on the front, and her jeans are looking shorter than the last time I brought her out. The combat boots—the same as mine—make me smile because she was so desperate to have them.

Mrs. Lancaster would have a coronary if she saw her dressed like this. She likes her in clothes that are sophisticated and clean: black pinafore dresses with the perfect crease ironed in them, shiny black patent shoes with not a scuff in sight, and her hair tied back with a black ribbon in it. She looks like she belongs in some sort of religious school.

Harper's hair, the exact same color as mine, blows in the breeze. The fact that she is a mini-me warms me. I'd love her no matter what, but knowing that she has more of me inside her than him gives me a sense of satisfaction.

"How about we get that ice cream now?" Cole's words cut through my thoughts.

"Cole, I don't think . . ."

"Please, Mommy?" Harper jumps off the swing and clasps her hands together as though saying a prayer.

"Me and peanut here have an understanding, don't we?" Cole raises an eyebrow at Harper.

Harper pulls her lips tight and makes a motion with her fingers, as though locking her lips together, forcing me to laugh when Cole mimics her actions.

I breathe out and smile. "Okay, fine."

"Eeek!" She bounces up and down on the balls of her feet. "I love you, Cole." Harper grabs his hand and then mine, and we walk together over toward the ice cream stand.

To anyone on the outside looking in, we'd look like the perfect little family taking their daughter out for the day, and I can't help but revel in it, if only for a short while. I can pretend we are just that, a family.

TEN

C ole

After taking Harper to feed the ducks down by the lake, we went to a café for lunch.

Harper and Tia ordered identical burgers, and I watched as they both mixed their mayo and ketchup together before dipping their fries into the mixture—I'm not even sure they realize it's something they both do. But I spent the afternoon embracing every second with them. The bond they have is blatant, something I'm sure the Lancasters are aware of and are no doubt jealous of.

Once we'd had lunch, Tia suggested we go to the local children's museum. Apparently, she takes Harper there a lot because the woman at the desk recognized them instantly.

Something tells me she goes there because you only have to make a donation to enter.

Watching Tia draw, with Harper sitting beside her mirroring her mom's actions, sent a pang to my chest. I always knew I wanted kids but never really considered when. But seeing them today, there isn't a doubt in my mind that they're mine. My girls.

My family.

Tia is gentle and patient with Harper, explaining how she highlights the pictures she's drawn by pressing harder on the pencil to make it stand out. Every few seconds, Tia's eyes would dart over toward Harper to check on her, even though she was literally sitting beside her. It was almost like she was scared someone was going to snatch her away. The thought made my jaw tic in annoyance. But the moment Harper smiled up at me with familiar eyes, my anger melted away.

Before we took Harper back to the Lancasters', Tia changed Harper back into the perfect-looking clothes. The lady on the desk puckered her lips and shook her head, as though she couldn't understand why anyone would want to dress a child to look like a shiny doll that you're unable to touch in case you mark it.

The car journey was solemn, with conversation between us all short and clipped. There was no way this kid was happy in that house; her short time with Tia only solidified what I already knew.

She needed to be back where she belonged. With Tia.

With us.

The nanny had greeted Harper when we arrived at the door. Even she had a look of sympathy oozing from her sharp eyes before turning and locking the door.

Tia gazes out the window all the way home, and when I notice a tear trickle down her cheek, my hands tighten on the steering wheel, so I rein in my temper; I refrain from slamming my hand onto the wheel and pressing down on the accelerator. Instead, I take deep breaths and remind myself Tia has to go through this every month. She literally has no control over her own child, a child who is becoming a puppet to a twisted bitch, and fuck only knows what her husband is like.

The thought that Tia had to battle this when she herself was only a child, I cannot imagine what strength and determination she must have. How she hasn't signed the papers for her adoption before now is a testament to that.

"You're an incredible mom, beauty." My voice is low, a whisper of how I feel. I want to scream and shout, tell her how amazing she is. Make her understand it.

She chuckles mockingly to herself. "I don't feel it, Cole."

"I get that."

She turns her head to face me, her eyes searching my face for truth. "They have the mansion, the money, the access to nice parks."

She nods at my words.

"You know what they don't have, beauty?" She stares at me with uncertainty in her eyes before shaking her head. "They don't have the bond you both have. They don't have what's in here." I tap my fist to my chest. "Love. You'd give that girl anything to make her happy, beauty. I saw that today. And if you think for one minute making her happy is money and what it brings with it, then you're lying to yourself."

Tears stream down her face.

"She loves you, beauty, with all her goddamn heart." My eyes flick back toward the road, then back to her.

"Besides, you have money now. Me and my brothers are loaded." I shrug and give her a smirk to lighten the mood.

She chokes on a chuckle of emotion, making me grin from ear to ear.

Damn fucking right she has me and my brothers now.

A strange wave of excitement and nervousness takes over me when I think of Tia living with my brothers.

We're going to be a family.

All of us.

TIA

I step into the bedroom after showering, feeling completely deflated like every time I return from having to kiss Harper goodbye; I feel empty, a shell.

My hair is wet and sticking to my face, and my towel is wrapped tightly around my body. I'm barely keeping myself together.

Cole is stretched out on my bed in only his boxer shorts. His head is propped up on his elbow, and he's watching me closely, as if sensing my impending meltdown.

"Come here, beauty." His voice oozes sympathy and comfort. Cole holds his arms out for me, and I walk toward him, letting him pull me into his solid chest as I fall against him.

I can't help the sob that catches in my throat. I've never had someone to cry into before, to offer me comfort, and right now, in his solid chest, I feel protected and cherished. I feel loved.

"I've got you. Let it out." My tears flow freely at his

words as his hand trails up and down my back. "Let it all out, beauty," he gently coos.

And I do, I cry until I can't cry anymore, until my eyes are empty of tears, and my mind is satiated, until I fall into the deepest sleep, where I dream of a life with Cole and Harper.

My own little family.

I can feel kisses being trailed down my spine, and wet lips gently suck at the flesh on my ass. Forcing my eyes open and down to the wet lips, Cole has his gaze firmly locked on mine. I roll onto my back to get a better view of him. His mouth parts as he takes in my naked body, exposed and suddenly desperate for him. His eyes are heavy and lust filled as I move my hand toward my clit, gently circling over the swollen bud of nerves.

"Are you going to put on a show for me, beauty?" His eyes flare as he watches me closely. He grips my thighs and opens me wide as he sits back on his heels to watch me from the bottom of the bed.

Cole's naked abs are taut in pleasure as he tugs on his length before stroking it to the same pace as my own movement.

His rhythm becomes reckless as his eyes flick from my fingers to my face. My spine arches as my climax nears. He moves his hips in time with his hand, fucking himself with vigor. It's one of the most erotic sights I've ever seen.

"Fuck, you're beautiful." His eyes hold mine hostage

as he says the words, giving me no option but to believe him. The way he looks at me makes me want to pull him close and never let him go. I want him to care for me, protect me, and love me.

"Please, Cole. I need you." His nostrils flare as I beg for him. "Please."

He licks his lips, causing a moan to escape me.

"Lick your fingers clean, beauty. Taste yourself."

I do as he asks, tasting my sweet essence. I suck on my fingers and close my eyes on a groan.

The bed shifts around me, and I open my eyes to find Cole lying beside me, his hard pierced cock leaking strings of pre-cum and standing to attention. "I want you to fuck me, beauty. I want to watch your tits bounce for me when you come on my thick cock."

I suck in a breath at his words. Rising from my position, I throw my leg over his solid body. My hands travel up his chiseled muscles, over the ridges of golden perfection. "Cole." His name comes out breathy, a whisper of need behind it.

Cole's cock sits beneath my wetness, and I slowly drag myself back and forth over him, relishing in the tight grip he has on my thighs as I rock against him.

"Beauty, you're teasing me."

My lips ghost over his. "I want you to fill me. To flood me with your cum."

His green eyes darken. "Fuck, I want that. I want your pussy to drown in my cum."

Our lips clash. His tongue forces itself in my mouth, and I stroke over his piercing, earning a groan of appreciation.

I continue to gently rock over his solid length, moaning when his pierced cock hits the perfect spot.

"Fuck, beauty, put me inside." Our mouths tangle together again, his tongue fucking my mouth as he bucks his hips up into me. "Put me inside, beauty." He groans ruggedly when I tighten my thighs on him, purposely ignoring him.

"Mmm, Cole. You feel so good."

"Fuck. Fuck, beauty." He grabs my hips and raises me, positions his cock, then slams me down on his full length without warning.

I throw my head back in both shock and pleasure, his thickness stretching me and his piercing rubbing against me. "Oh, Cole."

"Fuck yeah. Bounce on my cock, beauty."

I lift myself off his body and slam myself back down, over and over again.

"Fuck, let me see those tits."

I drag my hands roughly over my breasts, squeezing them together while Cole uses his grip on my thighs to raise me up and down. His hips buck into me with a slam from below. Wetness pools around me, a mixture of my arousal and his pre-cum flowing between us. "So fucking wet, beauty. So desperate for my cock."

"Yes. Please, Cole."

He leans forward and moves his hand to my breast, squeezing it as I hold it out for him. His tongue flicks over the peak of my nipple, the metal of his piercing sending a cold tremor through my body. He nips at me, grazing his teeth over the peak, causing me to wince before he gently kisses away the sting.

Cole drops back down onto the pillow. "Make love to me, beauty." His green eyes darken with a look of vulnerability about them, as though I'm about to reject his words. They echo in my mind. "Make love to me, beauty." And I've never wanted those words as much as I want them now. My chest tightens with the awareness. I nod in response, giving him what he wants, what we both want.

Love.

My pussy clenches as I gently move over his body. Our eyes stay locked in a silent stare, where we don't speak but say a million things at the same time.

"Cole, I . . ." My body tightens above his when I feel his muscles flex and his jaw locks, but our eyes stay on one another.

"I . . ." my breathing becomes ragged, and my heart hammers. My pussy squeezes him, pulling him closer. He continues to thrust up into me, but the grip on my thighs tells me he's refraining from working faster, harder. He's dragging this out; he's relishing in it as much as me.

"Fuck. I can't." He squeezes his eyes closed, and his nostrils flare before he darts his eyes open again, determination seeping from them. "Fuck. I . . ."

My pussy clamps around him as I squeeze my breasts tighter. Cole's lips part to speak, but I say it for him. I say the words.

"I love you."

He erupts deep inside me, but his hips continue moving at a languorous pace, and my pussy milks every drop of his thick cum.

"I love you too, beauty."

His cock still deep inside me, our release slides out as I drop onto his chest, my body and mind both spent.

"I can feel your cum dripping out of me." I giggle into his chest.

I feel him grin against my hair. "I need to plug that pussy." He breaks out into a chuckle, causing his chest to vibrate and my laugh to breeze over him. Cole tightens his arms around me, holding me close, as though I'd move from him at any second.

"I want you to move in with me." I still at his words, fear gripping me. This is not part of my plan; this is not what's meant to happen.

I'm meant to work, focus on school, and get Harper back.

"Shh, I can feel the panic in you, beauty." His hands tighten more. "I spoke to Lucas; he said our attorney suggested it. That it would look better for the custody case if you were living with the guy you were having a relationship with." His words come out rushed as though practiced but still full of nerves.

I turn my head to stare at him, and his green eyes ooze desperation, a plea. A promise.

"What about work?"

Cole's lips turn up in a smile. "Beauty, you don't have to work. I want to look after you."

My body tightens. I want to work; I need to work. I'm independent, I don't need handouts. Not anymore.

As if sensing my thoughts, he says, "But we have clubs. You can work in one of those. Bar work, administration. We're always hiring." He shrugs as though it's nothing, when in reality, it's taken me forever to gain employment. Yet, he's offering me a multitude of options.

"Beauty—" He licks his lips slowly. "I need to go home." He bends forward and presses a kiss to my forehead, holding my head to his lips. His fingers tighten in my hair. "Please. I don't want to lose you." He pulls back, and I see the sincerity in his eyes, the fear of losing us before we even get a chance to truly start.

"Please," he begs on a whisper.

My heart is in turmoil, a blend of fear and excitement for a new start.

A feeling of hope within reach.

"Okay," I agree on a soft smile.

Cole echoes my words with a huge grin. "Okay?"

I nod, my smile broadening, thanks to his enthusiasm.

"You won't regret it, beauty. I promise."

CHAPTER
ELEVEN

Lucas

My leg bounces with anxiety as Cole parks his truck in the underground carpark. When she gets out the car, I take her in, my heart hammering hard against my chest. She's here, she's finally here. My fingers twitch to touch her, to reach out and feel her silky hair between my fingers, to breathe in her scent.

Coconuts, that's what she'll smell like.

Cole's hand entwines with hers. He tugs her lovingly into his arms and gazes down at her with a wide smile playing on his lips. A pang of jealousy strikes me hard in the chest, but I'm not sure what I'm more jealous of: her soft smile of admiration back at him or the smile he gifts her with so much love in his eyes, it's obvious.

Obvious that they're meant to be.

I close the laptop lid with a slam and take it to my office. Placing it on the desk, my body stills as my eyes latch on to the drawer containing the files.

The elevator pings, snapping me out of my daze.

Time to meet our houseguest.

The giggling fills the apartment, a strange noise when it's normally so silent, so subdued.

She's smaller than I thought she would be, tucked perfectly under his arm with her arm tightly braced comfortingly and lovingly around his waist.

Both are completely unaware of my presence, and it annoys the hell out of me. The vein in my temple pulsates.

Did he not tell her about me at all?

I clear my throat and stare at them. My pulse races with annoyance, and my jaw twitches in aggravation.

Tia's head turns in my direction, and the air is sucked from my lungs. I grip the dining chair in front of me to stop myself from reaching her, from ripping her from his arms.

If only I was capable of that.

Tia wears ripped jeans that fit her like a glove, showcasing her curves. Her white T-shirt is tight across her chest, and I swear I can see her darkened nipples through her white bra.

Cole scrubs an awkward hand over his head. "Hey, man." He clears his throat. "This is Tia. Tia, this is my brother, Lucas."

"Hi. Nice to meet you, Lucas." She steps toward me and holds her hand out for me to take. I glare at it, willing myself to take it in mine.

Just fucking take it.

Cole chuckles. Breaking the tension mounting between us, he steps forward and takes Tia by the wrist. "Beauty. Lucas isn't into that kind of greeting." Her confused expression softens, as though she understands, and I hate it.

I hate that she might think I'm weird. Weak.

My airway feels like it's closing, and heat rises up my neck. The room feels like it's closing in on me. I move my hand inside my pocket to the security of my knife. My fingers stroke over the soft oak handle.

"I'm going out. Some of us have fucking work to do," I snap in Cole's direction, not willing to acknowledge the dejection in his eyes.

Cole can go to hell right now, for all I care.

He left me here for weeks to be with her. I stride toward the apartment door; I need to get out of here. I need to get away from him.

From both of them.

TIA

The door slams, making me jolt. "He hates me."

Cole pulls me into a protective hug and kisses the top of my head.

"He doesn't hate you, beauty. He's had a hard time and just doesn't know how to act around you. He'll come around."

I pull my head back to look at him. His eyes sparkle with truth, and a smile plays on his cocky lips.

"I need to fuck you so bad," he whispers breathily in my hair, making me turn fully to face him.

I nibble on my lip and glance around the immaculate apartment before turning back toward Cole. His gaze alight with excitement, he takes my hand and places it on his hard cock. My fingers brush over the length before he squeezes my hand against him.

"Here?" I question.

Cole only nods as he lowers himself to his knees, gently unbuttoning my jeans and dragging them down to my ankles before tugging them and my sneakers off in one go. He grips each side of my panties and tears them, leaving me exposed.

He picks me up and places me on the dining table. The coldness of the wood seeps into my bare skin, causing a tremor to rack through my body. The intensity of his glare penetrates me, causing my clit to throb in excitement.

He fumbles with his jeans and boxers, dropping them past his ass. His cock springs free with stickiness attached to the tip, making me squeeze him between my thighs as he steps closer toward me.

In one hard thrust, he's inside me, his piercing already hitting that perfect spot.

He withdraws fully and thrusts in hard again, and his fingers dig into my ass to keep me in place. I throw my head back when my pussy clenches around him.

"Your tits, beauty." He pants as he hammers into me, my pussy holding on for dear life. "Give me your tits."

I scramble to free myself, unhooking my bra and pulling up my shirt for him. "Ah god, Cole. Please. I need your mouth on them, please," I beg and pull his face toward my nipple, relishing and moaning when he latches on to the stiffened peak. I hold his head in place as his piercing flicks over the tender bud. A sucking noise leaves his throat, as though he can't get enough of me, causing wetness to gather around us.

Without warning, Cole pushes me down against the cold wood of the table, and with one hand, he grips my throat. His hips work faster, and his free hand breezes over my clit, circling it gently. The action drives me wild.

"Holy shit, beauty." Sweat coats his forehead. "I'm going to come inside you. Fuck yes."

He presses my clit harder as his pierced tongue circles my nipple.

His thrusts become faster, and my pussy contracts, making my juices flood from inside me. "Cole, I . . ." I arch my back, pushing his head harder against me. The scrape of his teeth ignites the inferno building inside. "Yes!" I erupt around him, sending him spiraling too.

"Fuck, beauty. Take my cum. Take all my cum in your tight little pussy." He swells and then I feel the ropes of his cum hitting my walls, coating me with him.

His head drops into the crook of my neck, our hearts hammering together. I grip him closer. "I love you," I whisper into his ear.

He pulls back. Searching my face, his expression softens, and a smile graces his lips. "I love you too, beauty." Cole snaps his eyes up, looking straight above me. The action is odd and causes me to turn to see where he's looking. Nothing, he's looking at nothing.

The hairs on my neck stand up, and a lump forms in my throat, an odd sensation I don't feel often anymore.

Strange.

"Shall I show you to our room?" he queries with a raised eyebrow.

"Sure."

"Come on, beauty, let's get you settled."

I hop down off the table with cum trickling down my thighs. Cole smirks in my direction, making me playfully push him.

"You're such an ass."

"Yeah, I am. And you love me for it." He grins, nuzzling kisses down my neck as he opens the door to his bedroom.

Our bedroom.

TWELVE

Cole

After showing Tia the ginormous bathroom, I went in search of Lucas. I'd heard a door slam down the hall and knew he was back and no doubt stewing.

Opening his office door, I step inside without knocking. His eyes snap up to meet mine from above his computer.

"I've ordered Chinese, and we're going to watch a movie. Are you going to join us?"

He pauses and stares at me with such intensity, I shuffle uncomfortably on the spot. I hate it when he does this, withdraws from me. "Come on, Lucas. Don't be like this." I wince at the pleading tone in my voice.

Lucas's gray eyes drill into mine. He's pissed, but I'm not even sure why.

Before he finally exhales, the silence between us is deafening.

"I haven't seen you in weeks." He spits the words out with vitriol. "You left." His words hang in the air.

I left and came back with someone, someone I love. Possibly more than him. He thinks it but refuses to say it.

"Then you fuck her on the dining table you expect me to eat at?" His cold eyes should unnerve me, but they don't. I'm used to his unfeeling, detached demeanor.

I chuckle to myself. "I knew you'd be watching. I thought you'd like that." I grin at the gift I handed to him on a silver platter, fresh material for his spank bank. "Next time, I'll make sure she faces the other way. You should see her come, brother." My cock swells in my jeans at the mere thought. Lucas doesn't miss the action either; his eyes flick to my cock, then quickly back up to my face as though completely unfazed.

If he could just give in . . .

"I'm not hungry." He snaps his mouth shut, making me scoff at his juvenile attitude.

"Sure you're not. You can sit here pretending you don't want a taste of my girl's pussy all you like, but we both know you do."

I turn on my heel and make my way into the kitchen.

If only he would give in.

Everything would be perfect.

TIA

I set the plates on the table. A ripple of excitement runs through me. This feels like home. I've only been here a matter of hours, and already, this feels like home.

The open-plan space is vast, with overly large couches filling the living area, and a huge television, far bigger than any I've seen before, is on the wall.

The floor-to-ceiling windows overlook a park, and my heart swells at the thought of bringing Harper here. Is this something even achievable? I bite my bottom lip, deep in thought. I can only hope what Cole is promising me will one day transpire.

"Hey, beauty. You good?" Cole's rough hands wrap around my waist from behind, and he kisses into my neck, making me squirm and giggle on the spot.

I place the final set of cutlery down and turn to face him. He eyes the table with a look of longing. Maybe he's missing his other brother, Rage. "He's home in just under two weeks, right?" I question him.

His eyes flick up to mine in confusion.

"Rage."

He jolts. "Oh yeah. Two weeks. Lucas won't be joining us." He waves his hand at the table, and my shoulders deflate, knowing that Lucas is the cause of his disappointment, not Rage's absence.

From the moment I locked eyes with Lucas, I knew he instantly didn't like me. Despite the fact that he was dressed to perfection—wearing a white shirt tucked into belted black pants that fit his fine ass perfectly—he glared at me with contempt, a look of disgust in his eyes, gleaming in spite.

Lucas has olive skin, broad shoulders—although smaller than Cole—and he must be a similar height, maybe a little shorter than Cole, but only just. Lucas's eyes are an odd color, almost gray looking; they make him all the more intriguing, yet weary too. His thick dark hair is short on the sides but longer on top and brushed back. He reminds me of someone with an Italian heritage; he has a dark Mafia vibe about him that tangles me in a web of excitement yet leaves me with a ball of nervousness.

He watches me like a hunter watching its prey; every movement of his eyes was calculated to scrutinize me, analyze my actions—no doubt judging my intentions with Cole.

My stomach did a nervous flip when his eyes latched on to my chest, causing heat to travel up my neck and my feet to shuffle awkwardly on the spot.

Cole told me little about his brothers other than the fact that Lucas has a troubled past, and Rage spends his time taking out his aggression in the fight clubs they own if not in a different girl's bed every night.

When Lucas rejected my outstretched hand, I wasn't surprised. I can't imagine he'd want to touch me with the disgust he harbors toward me. And when Cole reminded me of his reasons behind the lack of enthusiasm, I wanted to kick myself. I've been there. I should know the aftereffects of trauma when I see it.

I live it every day.

THIRTEEN

L ucas

    I can hear them in the living area. My hands tremble with a need to open my laptop and watch them together. I wonder if Cole is giving me another show?

When I watched him fuck her earlier, it was just as incredible as I imagined. The longing in his eyes, the utter desire swimming from them.

He fucked her hard and fast, his fingers digging into her ass cheeks. I wonder if she has his imprint on them?

I wonder if he's marked her?

I'd like my mark on her too. Something permanent. Something that shows she belongs to me as much as she belongs to him.

My cock twitches against my boxers as I imagine him fucking her, Tia moaning for more, holding his head tight to her breast.

Fuck, they're beautiful together.

His bedroom door handle clicks, making my ears

perk as I listen out for them, wishing for once the walls were thinner than they actually are. I stand from my bed, my solid cock peeking from under the waistband of my boxers.

Walking toward my already open bedroom door, I step into the dark corridor.

Cole and I sleep with our doors open, him so he can hear me if I have a bad episode in the night and me so that I know he's there if I need him—so I know I'm not being locked away, unable to escape.

They're moaning against one another, and my hand twitches to push his door open even more, just a little. My heart races at the thought. I wonder what she feels like.

What *it* feels like.

When she screams out his name, my cock pulsates on its own accord, forcing me to move into the living area away from them, swallowing away the shame of wanting them.

I find myself standing at the dining table, looking down at the exact spot he fucked her at earlier. My hand glides over the wood where her firm ass was sitting.

Where her pussy was being pounded by him.

I take my cock out and point it over the bare wood, wiping the pre-cum over the exact spot her perfect pussy cried out for him to fuck her harder. The cold wood against my tip sends a shiver of excitement through my body.

I fist myself tighter, roughly pumping my cock over the table. Fucking her harder, faster. Forcing her to take my thick cock.

My orgasm hits me hard, and it forces me onto my tiptoes. "Fuck!" Ropes of thick white cum splash onto the woodwork, marking it.

Marking this spot as mine too.

I STRAIGHTEN MY CUFFLINK, a nervous feeling taking over my stomach that I don't like. It's because of her.

Cole is at the gym this morning, and I can hear her in the kitchen, our kitchen. Hers now too.

Stepping into the corridor, I take a deep breath and steeple my emotions behind the façade I let people see every day.

Arrogance, confidence, and control.

As if sensing my approach, she turns. Her lips part, but no words leave them. Her cheeks pinken, and I can't help but wonder why. Does she find me attractive? My heart hammers against my chest.

Her blue eyes quickly flick over my frozen form before glancing away and back at the countertop. Disappointment curdles inside me, her look of appreciation short lived.

Placing my laptop on the dining table, I walk toward the refrigerator, ignoring her completely.

The atmosphere between us is cold and detached.

I take out a shake and open the bottle, take a glass from the cupboard, and pour it in. Drinking the shake in one go, I rinse the glass and place it into the dishwasher. Then, I move toward the coffee maker and begin to make myself a cup.

"Would you like a croissant? They're freshly made."

I glance around at the mess on the counter and cringe. My hands tighten on my mug while I tell myself she'll clean it once she's finished.

Her eyes dart toward the mess. "I'll tidy it up, Lucas. I wouldn't leave it like this."

Her soft voice sends a bolt of longing and need through me, forcing me to take a seat at the dining table to hide my growing erection.

I open the laptop as an attempt to distract me from her. Conscious of her presence, I try my best to ignore her by swiping up at today's calendar to view the meetings with my legal team.

"The croissant, would you like one?"

I refuse to glance up and see the light extinguish from her eyes when I utter the word "No" in the same sharp tone I use for business meetings.

She sighs heavily before turning back around and continuing whatever she's doing with the croissant.

I never eat breakfast. Even after moving into Cole's house, I still couldn't stomach it after going without it for so long.

I watch her from over the top of my laptop. She makes quick work of tidying the kitchen, then takes her plate and seems to hover around the dining table, unsure whether to sit or not. My eyes latch on to hers, making her gaze dart away. "I'm taking this to Cole's room." She holds up the plate with the croissant.

Annoyance rumbles inside me. Does she not want to be in my presence?

"Sit!" I snap and nod toward the chair opposite me, the same space I fucked my hand to last night.

She slowly places the plate down on the table, as though I'm a predator and she's my prey, her movements uncertain.

The plate sits in the exact spot I came all over last night, the same place her hands now rest. I imagine my cum seeping into her skin from beneath her hand. The thought alone makes me close my eyes and breathe steady breaths through my nostrils.

"Lucas. If me being here bothers you . . ."

I snap my eyes open. Vulnerability and hurt coat her expression, and her shoulders are slumped forward.

"It doesn't bother me." I hold her gaze, hoping she can see the truth behind my words.

"I want to thank you, for everything that you're doing for me and Harper." Our eyes connect, and the atmosphere between us is so tense she darts her eyes away.

"I'm going for full custody. But it might take a while, so for now, I'm pushing for more visitation," I say.

Her body practically vibrates with excitement, and my lips turn up at her reaction. "You are?"

I try to mask how warm and proud I feel inside that I caused that reaction. Instead, I give her a firm nod. "I am. She deserves to be with her mother, and Cole says you're incredible with Harper."

A wistful look takes over her face, and she breaks off a piece of the croissant, placing it on her tongue. I watch the movement of her mouth, transfixed. "I won't hurt him. I would never." She flicks her tongue over her lip, taking the small crumb sitting there with it.

I swallow past the lump in my throat, my cock rock hard in my pants and pressing painfully against my zipper. My eyes dart down toward the table; the marking is still there but not visible to someone unaware.

"I promise." Her voice seeps through my skin and into my heart.

I want to believe it.

But when she finds out the secrets I'm withholding, will she feel the same way? Will she punish him?

Will Tia choose him above everything else?

FOURTEEN

T ia

    Since the incident at breakfast four days ago, I can now move around the apartment with a feeling of relative ease.

There's a comfortable silence between me and Lucas. I can feel him watching me, and if I was being completely honest with myself, I can't say I hate it. I enjoy his presence; it's like a blanket of protection wrapped around me at all times.

Lucas works mainly from the apartment, bringing his laptop into the living area while I work on my drawings. Often, I have a sense of awareness, and my pulse races. I'm convinced I can feel his eyes on me, but whenever I glance his way, he's always working.

He rarely goes out, only when he's needed at meetings.

Then, when Cole is home, he tends to back away and move into his office to give us space, but I feel his absence instantly, like a dull ache, and I long for him to be near.

I snuggle into Cole further, my head resting in his lap and my body curled up on my side, laying on the couch as we both watch an action movie play out on the huge television screen.

I feel him before I see him. The hairs on my skin stand to attention at his perusal of me. I instantly become aware of my ass cheeks peeking out of my pajama shorts and the camisole top that's risen too high and now sits just under my breasts, exposing my stomach.

I glance his way; he's standing, watching me, his eyes latched on to my ass cheeks. I suck in a sharp breath, unable to hide my reaction to him, and my chest heats at the thought.

He looks edible. His bare chest is still wet from showering, low gray joggers fall on the perfect ridged V with a scattering of dark hair leading down into the waistband.

He swallows thickly as my eyes meet his, and his hand tightens around his beer bottle, forcing the cords of his forearm muscles to bulge.

My nipples pebble under his scrutiny, and I swear his gray eyes darken with the knowledge of them doing so. My heart races, and the flush travels up to my face, making me suddenly grateful for the dim lighting.

"Brother, stop perving on my girl and come sit down." Cole chuckles, breaking the sexual tension radiating from us.

I try to act unperturbed, brushing the hair from my

face and shuffling slightly to ease the wetness I feel gathering between my legs from Lucas's intense stare.

"Beauty, it's okay. Lucas can squeeze in, can't you?"

My eyes dart to Lucas as he slowly approaches like a wounded animal, clearly unsure of himself. His eyes swim with nervousness, making me want to pull him closer and tell him he's welcome, that he can join us.

My pulse races at the thought before a pang of guilt hits me, cooling me down in an instant.

"Tia can rest her legs on you." I glance toward Cole, a confident and smooth expression on his face. Not at all giving way to even the slightest bit of unease or showing that he's picked up on any tension between the two of us, he motions for Lucas to sit down at the end of the couch.

I stare at the television, trying not to think of Cole's huge body against my small one—overshadowing me —and now Lucas at the base of the couch, who flinches slightly when I rest my feet in his lap.

I go to move them away, but his voice comes out a choked whisper. "It's okay."

I swallow past the lump in my throat at his words, the warmth of his legs traveling through his joggers and onto my feet.

I cast a glance at him. He's staring straight at the wall, not even looking at the television. His body is frozen still, and he's tightly gripping the beer bottle. His shoulder muscles are pulled tight as he sits stoically still, as though he's afraid to move.

Cole begins trailing his hand up and down my arm,

sending a trail of goose bumps over my body. My heart races, and my nipples pebble beneath my top.

Lucas side-eyes the motion and eases himself into the cushions as though having to mentally force himself to relax.

His hand hovers over my foot with an evident tremble. My heart aches for him. Clearly, he wants to be included, but he's either unsure of how far to go or unable to give in. Something inside me tells me it's the latter, that he's desperate to give in, that he wants a physical relationship, but he doesn't know how or won't allow himself.

My mind wanders, thinking about the little I know about Lucas other than Cole telling me he comes from a bad background of trauma, and that's when I make my decision for him. I lift my foot and nudge his hand. His eyes dart toward mine in a widened panic, as though he's done something wrong. I nod toward my foot and nudge his hand again, letting him know I want him to place his hand on my foot, touch it, caress it, just hold it.

Hold me.

I settle back into Cole with the soft glide of Lucas's hand on my skin, setting alight a thousand tingles over my bare flesh.

Cole bends down low to my ear. "Good girl, beauty."

His words make me squirm on the spot, my sleep shorts feeling wetter than ever before.

As if realizing my turned-on state, Cole moves his hand over my shoulder and toward my breast, slowly rotating his thumb over the material, stroking me to the point of distraction. His thumb brushes over my nipple and caresses it, making my pussy clench at his touch.

Cole thrusts slightly against me. The hardness of his cock by my face makes my breath quicken and my body heat as I struggle with my thoughts, unable to decide where to direct them: over the tender stroke of Lucas's hand on my foot or over the pleasurable caress of my nipple from Cole's fingers.

A moan of contentment escapes my lips, causing Cole to chuckle. "Come on, beauty. I think you need some attention. Let's get you in bed."

I don't miss the disappointment washing over Lucas's face, nor the slump in his shoulders.

Guilt clouds my vision as I stand with my hand entwined with Cole's. I can't look at him, not when I encouraged his touch and now I'm taking it away.

But as I turn and move away from the couch, my eyes latch on to the unmistakable solid erection in his joggers with a very prominent wet spot.

Did Lucas get hard just through touching me?

And why the hell am I so turned on by that when I'm so in love with Cole?

When I should feel guilt, all I feel is an overwhelming urge to please them.

Both of them.

CHAPTER
FIFTEEN

Tia

Cole holds my pussy open and licks my folds, forcing my back to arch in pleasure. His thick fingers push forcefully inside me, rubbing that perfect spot. He rubs his face from side to side, his day-old scruff adding a fraction of friction to my sensitive pussy and heightening my need for him more.

"Please," I beg as my hand meets his head to hold him in place.

He flicks his piercing over my clit and latches on to it, sucking it into his mouth.

"Oh fuck." I explode on his tongue, my muscles clenching around his fingers, holding him deep inside me. Slowly, my body relaxes below him.

"Fuck. That was hot, beauty." He sits up on his knees, staring down at me with my arousal on his face. He pulls on his cock roughly in one hand, his piercing shining under the low lighting, making me lick my lips at the thought of playing with it in my mouth and making him groan in appreciation.

A shadow moves in the doorway. It's been happening the past few days, and the thought of knowing Lucas is just beyond the doorway sends my need for him into overdrive. Hoping he can see me naked for Cole adds to my arousal.

Cole insists on keeping the door ajar in case Lucas needs anything during the night, another insight into Lucas's past that still haunts him today.

I freeze when Lucas steps into the room, his muscled body coiled tight, his jaw locked, and his eyes trained on us.

Both of us.

Cole glances over his shoulder, then scans my face. "You okay with Lucas watching, beauty?"

I search his face for a moment, unable to convey my words, his words whirling around in my head. *You okay with Lucas watching, beauty?* Am I? Am I okay with the man I'm so intrigued with watching us?

As if sensing my inner battle, Cole takes the decision out of my hands. "Sit." He nods toward the armchair located in the corner of the room, positioned at an angle facing the bed, and for a moment, I wonder if it's been done strategically.

Lucas licks his lips and brushes a hand through his hair as though filled with trepidation. My eyes latch on to his joggers, his cock visibly hard. I shuffle below Cole, suddenly eager to have his cock fill me, fill the ache I feel for both him and Lucas.

Our eyes stay on Lucas as he sits stoically still on the

chair, his legs spread wide and his hands gripping the chair tightly, the whites of his knuckles gleaming in the light.

"Should I put my thick cock inside her?" He stares at Lucas for approval.

Lucas swallows thickly and fidgets. His gray eyes are dark and intense, and he stares at my face, as though Cole doesn't exist.

He clears his throat. "Is she wet?"

Cole chuckles. "So fucking wet. I ate her out, and she came on my tongue. Tastes so good, brother." He pants with glee.

Lucas's eyes dart toward Cole's cocky smile, trailing his gaze over his face, then down his body to his hard cock standing with glistening pre-cum on the tip.

"Push it in slow." He grunts the words out as though forced. "Choke her while you do it."

Lucas shuffles forward, his hands still tight on the chair, as though forcing himself to stay seated.

Cole's hand latches onto my neck, and his lips dust over mine. "Such a good girl, beauty, letting my brother watch us as I fuck your little pussy."

I moan at his words, and his fingers tighten on my throat, just as his thick cock pushes past my entrance.

"Are you fucking her raw?" Lucas's voice comes out choked in disbelief.

"Yeah."

He mumbles a "Jesus" as though he's transfixed at the thought, and his lips part.

"Fuck. You feel good." Cole thrusts his hips forward. "Mmm, so good." His mouth falls open in pleasure, and a look of euphoria coating his features makes me clench his cock tighter in pleasure.

"Her tits. Play with her tits." Lucas's heady voice fills the room between Cole's grunts and my moans.

Cole's hand leaves my throat as he sits back slightly. Staring down at my tits, he pushes them together, tweaking the nipples between his fingers.

"Fuck, that looks amazing." Lucas rests forward on his elbows, his face trained on Cole's hands pushing my tits together. My necklace rests between them as he massages his fingers over my nipples, earning him a satisfying moan from my lips.

"More," I beg.

"Do it. Suck on her nipple, pull it tight."

I throw my head back in ecstasy as his lips lock around my nipple. His tongue flicks over my peak, and he sucks it hard into his wet mouth. I grip the bed sheets, balling them in my fists.

"Hold his head, Tia. Force him on your tit." My mouth drops open, and my pussy begins to clench. Cole hammers into me harder and harder as my hand locks around his head, holding him to my tit. He bites my nipple, then quickly sucks away the sting. Using my other hand, I claw at his back, frantically digging my nails in.

The bed hits the wall over and over again with the power behind Cole's movements.

I meet his thrusts; his cock begins to pulsate.

I raise my hips into him, and his movements stutter.

"Fuck her harder, Cole. Harder!" Lucas barks in annoyance.

I latch onto his eyes, his wide in awe. His hips move against his joggers, clearly rubbing his erection against the material for friction, and his chest is heaving up and down in excitement.

When I feel Cole's cock burst with cum, I scream out my orgasm.

"Oh god, yes!"

My gaze is on Lucas and his slackened jaw, his body suddenly rigid.

Did he just come?

A tremor works through me at the thought, sending a thousand tingles over my body, along with a flutter of need.

Need for him.

COLE

I pepper kisses over my girl. By far, this has been the most incredible experience of my life, and her allowing Lucas to join us in it only cements the fact that we're perfect together.

All of us.

I've never felt the need to share the girl I'm fucking before now, and never have I considered having a relationship with a man. But this is Lucas, my brother. And he needs this as much as me. More than me.

I trust her, and in return, so does Lucas.

I've seen the want and need oozing from his eyes, his erection growing behind his pants whenever she's near.

He's always enjoyed watching from the shadows, desperate to step into the room but never actually doing it. The excitement of knowing he's there and craving what I have has never bothered me until now. Until her.

Because now, I want to share what I feel. I want him to experience everything Tia has to offer: her love, her support, and her pussy. And something tells me she wants it too.

I've seen her eyes track his movement before she guiltily looks away, the way her throat bobs in uncertainty and heat rises to her cheeks when he sits near her.

Lucas doesn't realize how much attention he's been giving her, and when I thought she would run, cower from his blatant obsession with her, she didn't.

I've no doubt her panties have been getting wetter at the thought of having my brother as much as me, and I revel in it. My cock hardens inside her. Even after emptying such a big load, it wants to go again.

It's him. His eyes on her.

On us.

I move my hips again, letting her feel my solid cock.

"Are you hard?" His deep voice sends a wave of excitement to my balls.

I'd never realized having someone instruct me on sex was such a turn on, someone to dominate me.

Us.

"Yeah."

"Pull out and fuck her throat."

The gruffness behind his voice makes me stumble to pull out. Cum drips from my cock as I move, positioning myself over her. With my legs on either side of her head, I kneel above her.

Tia's mouth opens on instinct, and before I get a chance to think about what I'm doing, I hit the back of her throat roughly. I grip the headboard with both fists and start hammering into her mouth, not stopping when she begins to choke.

"Don't stop. Don't stop, she likes it." Lucas's voice becomes ragged, and I glance over my shoulder to see him fucking his hand wildly. Oh shit, that's hot.

I glance down at my cock, shoving in and out of her mouth. Her eyes are wide, but there's not an ounce of fear in them. No, they're filled with lust. She's loving this as much as me. As much as him. Sweat coats my body, and my muscles pull tight from the force of ramming into her.

I clench my ass cheeks to ward off my impending orgasm.

"Fuck. Such a whore for my cock, beauty." The words tumble from my mouth, and I smirk when she moans around my cock, the vibration hitting my piercing and sending me spiraling.

"Fuck. I'm—" My words catch in my throat when Lucas's roar summons my own.

I flood her mouth with my cum, making her choke on my essence.

My head drops forward, and I gently pull my cock from her mouth. She sucks on the tip as though relishing the taste of me.

"Fuck. That was hot," Lucas comments from behind me.

I laugh awkwardly, unsure what to do now as I climb off Tia.

Lucas tucks his cock away and quickly stands, looking everywhere but at either of us. He darts toward the door, leaving me standing here with my cock out and Tia exposed, as though he didn't just play a part in it.

"Give him time, Cole." Her soft voice makes me turn,

and suddenly, I feel anxious. Will I lose her because we did this? Did she even want it? Did she get caught up in the moment and now regrets it?

"You're overthinking things. I can see it on your face." She nibbles on her lip, then bends to pull the sheets open. "Come on." She nods toward the bed, making my shoulders relax with the knowledge we're good.

I climb into the bed and cover us with the sheets. Tia instantly wraps her arms around my shoulders and throws a leg over my groin, drawing herself into me as close as she can get. I squeeze her tighter to me and kiss her hair. "You know I love you, right?" I ask her, with nervousness in my tone that makes me want to wince.

She draws back to look at me, not a hint of uncertainty in her eyes. "Of course."

I swallow thickly. "Was it okay?" I struggle to look at her. "What we just did, I mean."

Tia giggles. "It was more than okay."

My muscles relax with her words.

"It was hot, Tia." I wiggle my eyebrows in jest to lighten the moment. The action makes her nudge me playfully.

"Have you done anything like that before?" She nibbles her lip with vulnerability.

"No. I know he's watched a few times from the door, but he's never been in the room before. Sure as fuck never told me what to do," I joke in shock.

"You liked it." It's a statement from her lips that I can't argue with, so I nod in agreement but don't voice how much I did like it. How much I want it again. Want him.

I stroke the loose strands of her golden hair from her beautiful face. The light shines onto a few of her freckles, making her look younger than she actually is. Fuck me, she's beautiful.

"He doesn't have experience, beauty." A lump gathers in my throat, making it difficult for me to speak, to admit Lucas's truth. "Not the type of experience he wants."

Her eyes shine with understanding, and her body coils tight, forcing me to pull her closer, to protect her from her own demons.

Maybe that's why there's such a connection between them both. They both have experienced the darkest of traumas, but both hold a light in their eyes. One that connects them, that shines brighter than the flames of hell.

"I liked it." Her breath is a whisper as she snuggles into my chest.

"I felt your pussy clench every time he spoke."

She nods against my chest as I stroke her hair. "I don't want to lose you," she whispers.

"That'll never happen, beauty. You're mine."

My heart hammers in my chest as I prepare to say the words, prepare to admit how I feel and what I want.

"I love you, Tia."

She squeezes me tighter and places a tender kiss over my heart.

"I love you too, Cole."

A ball of emotion clogs in my throat.

"You're mine, Tia. You both are."

She sinks into me, and I can feel the trace of her smile against me.

"You both are," I repeat with conviction.

Now, I just need to get Lucas onboard, let him see how amazing we can become.

The three of us.

CHAPTER
SIXTEEN

Lucas

"We're going out for dinner." Cole stands in the doorway of my office with his arms crossed over his broad chest and his jaw clenching. No doubt, his pissed off expression is because of my absence the past few days.

I've made myself scarce. I've withdrawn from them both and struggled with thoughts of losing them, a combination of embarrassment, awkwardness, and downright terror of the fucked-up situation I've found myself in.

I know what I want, but I don't know how to get it, and the thought of hurting either one of them feels too much to bear.

A pang of fear hits me hard, and my breath hitches in a desperate need to gain air.

"You're coming with us," he tacks on, completely missing my internal meltdown.

His words sink into me. *"You're coming with us."* They want me.

They both want me.

"W-What?" I remain frozen, unsure of his meaning.

"Dinner. We're leaving in half an hour." He glances at his watch in annoyance. "Go shower or something. You look like shit."

He turns and walks away, leaving me with no option but to push my chair back and do as he instructs.

She looks beautiful. A small red dress barely covers her luscious ass and molds to her body perfectly. Her blonde waves flow down her back, and when she turns toward me, my footing wavers. Her eyes latch on to mine, tugging my heart and gripping it like a vise. She licks her blood-red lips, and excitement skitters down my spine at the thought of marking her to match her dress. Marking her with blood.

The thought should sicken me, repulse me beyond comprehension, but instead, it makes my cock stiffen in my pants and my hand search for my knife, gripping it tightly in my palm, stroking it with excitement.

"Finished with your pity party, then?" Cole saunters into the living area, eyeing me like a snake, his eyes seething and his jaw tight with tension. I stand taller, ignoring his taunts, feigning confidence and swallowing away the guilt.

"Tia's been worried about you!" He spits the words out like poison, and my eyes dart to hers in question.

She shrugs with a delicate smile placed there to make me feel at ease.

My heart rattles. It wants to run, and the meager contents in my stomach threaten to expel to the floor. I hurt her.

And with the look of hate piercing through Cole's eyes?

I hurt both of them.

I wince and squeeze my eyes closed as a swell of panic bubbles inside me. "Lucas. It's okay. Really, it's okay now." Her soft hand touches my spine and mimics her delicate tone. My fist tightens on my knife for security. She's touching me.

"Can we just go out and enjoy the evening?" she asks, her eyes jumping from mine to Cole's.

He seems to finally grasp the intensity of my panic; his face relaxes and fills with sympathy, forcing my eyes away from his, unable to deal with his assumptions.

"Let's go." His deep voice cuts through the air, leaving no room for negotiation as he marches toward the elevator.

I follow behind them, my hand twitching to touch her, hold her hand in mine. But instead, she holds Cole's.

She is his, after all.

TIA

Having the attention of two men on me is something I thought I'd never be comfortable with, but in all honesty, it feels liberating.

I flourish in the knowledge that Cole looks like he's seconds away from ripping my clothes off, yet Lucas appears controlled. But the sharpness of his jaw and the grinding of his teeth each time the waiter approaches the table leads me to believe he's just as affected.

"She rode my face like a champ on a bucking bronco." Cole grins, making me choke on my wine. What the fuck?

The waiter stumbles as he pours the water. Then, he quickly continues, with a flush traveling up his neck.

Lucas's eyes darken and slowly turn toward Cole with a deadly glare.

"Tastes so fucking good." He sticks his tongue out, the piercing taunting Lucas as he wiggles it around mockingly.

"Shut up," Lucas seethes back. The waiter's eyes flick

between the two of them, playing a deadly game with one another.

Cole chuckles. "You don't know what you've been missing." He glances up toward the waiter. "Our girl has been begging for your cum, Lucas. You just need to feed it to her. Isn't that right, beauty?"

I shuffle in my chair, a combination of embarrassment at Cole's blunt words in the waiter's presence and arousal at the thought of Lucas joining us once again.

"I made her call your name while I fucked her." His grin encompasses his smug face.

Lucas's nostrils flare, and in a move I don't see coming, he strikes, launching across the table. A bone-crunching crack pierces the air when his fist collides with Cole's jaw.

"Oh shit." I jump up from my chair and move toward them.

Lucas takes a step back as soon as I touch his shoulder. All the tension is suddenly gone, like a switch has been pressed by my simple touch.

"Are you okay?" I ask him, my eyes searching his with concern.

He nods while checking his knuckles. "Yeah."

"You could have broken my fucking jaw!" Cole springs up from his chair.

"Cole, enough!" He stops in his tracks. "You're taunting him. Now leave him alone."

Cole rolls his eyes. "If he broke my jaw, you wouldn't be able to ride my face, beauty." He smirks, appearing completely undaunted at the recent scuffle. "Who would eat you out?" He raises an eyebrow toward Lucas daringly.

Lucas appears to be doing some deep breathing technique. "Guess you'd have to find another man to fulfill your needs," he adds.

Lucas's eyes flare open, and he takes a step to go around me.

I put my hand on his arm to stop him and stand on my tiptoes. His hand ghosts around my back, holding me in place. "He's playing with you, Lucas. Don't pay him any attention. I only want you and Cole."

He seems to ease at my words before scanning my face for truth. I can't help myself. I move without thinking, placing a delicate kiss to the corner of his mouth.

His body freezes, and I take a step back, realizing I've overstepped. He clears his throat before moving behind me. Bracing his hands on the table, he covers my back with his chest, yet only faintly touching me. His breath hits my ear, causing goose bumps to break out across my skin. "Thank you." His voice is as low as a whisper, as smooth as silk and as hot as hell.

Lucas moves away from me, but not before grazing my ass with his solid cock. He rubs it along my ass cheek with accuracy.

He wants me to know he's hard.

He wants me to want him. My breath hitches, and I practically pant with need.

"Come on, beauty. Let's get you home and get that pussy fed." Cole winks in my direction, sending a thrill through my body, and the waiter's tray tumbles to the floor.

CHAPTER
SEVENTEEN

Cole

As soon as we step foot inside the apartment, I'm on her like a wild animal. I push up her dress and free my cock from my jeans with vigor.

Seeing Lucas dressed up for her made me hungry for them both, her to fuck and him to fuck with. The intense arousal at the thought of my brother wanting her as much as I do makes my cock ache with desperation.

I pepper messy kisses down her neck.

"Mark her," he snaps from beside me. He's standing so close I can smell his cologne, the one I bought him last Christmas, the one he knows I like.

I tug her skin between my teeth and pull savagely. A gasp of pain leaves her lips, but when I scan her face, all I see is arousal.

Tia grabs my face in one hand and pulls my open mouth to hers, sucking on my tongue, toying with my piercing eagerly.

"Beauty," I pant the word out, unsure of the reason, just because.

The moment my hand reaches my cock, my eyes close in pleasure.

"Get it out, let us see," Lucas hisses beside me.

I flick my eyes toward his, his transfixed on us both. His solid erection protrudes from his dress pants.

Let us see. His words echo in my mind. He said us. He wants us. Both of us. The thought sends my balls throbbing, and my cock begins to leak pre-cum.

I drop my jeans and boxers, sending them down to my feet. I flick off my shoes and socks and kick my clothes to the side. Tia pulls my top over my head, and now I'm fully naked. Every muscle and ridge is tight with need for her. And him.

"Fuck," he hisses through his teeth, making me have the sudden urge to hoist Tia up against the wall and plunge into her wet heat. Her head falls back against the wall as I begin pounding into her tight little pussy.

"Fuck, that's it. Fuck her hard."

"Jesus. You like that, Lucas? You like watching me fuck our woman hard?" I pant the words out as I grind my cock into her.

"More," she begs.

I grip her throat, knowing that turns him on, and on hearing his belt buckle clang, my balls draw up, making me squeeze my eyes shut and forcing my movements to stutter, hoping my orgasm doesn't happen just yet.

I thrust up hard into her, and my piercing rubs her favorite spot, making her respond by clenching around me.

"That's it, fuck her." He spits the words out with malice.

I concentrate on my girl—our girl—as I fuck her senseless. Her nails dig into my shoulders as she clings to me, her pussy saturating my cock.

"Dirty girl likes to be fucked while my brother watches," I whisper in her ear.

Tia grips my cock harder, her muscles pulling me in.

"You like being watched. Getting fucked like a whore." I nip at her ear.

"Her tits." I hear him swallow hard. "Play with her tits."

"Fuck, Lucas. I've only got two fucking hands. Come play with them yourself," I snap back at him.

I hear him fumbling beside me, making me snap my eyes toward him. My shoulders slacken slightly when I see him buckle his belt back up.

His eyes meet mine, darkness and anger radiating from them. Holy fucking shit. I've never seen him so pissed.

My movements have stopped completely, and a tremble works over Tia's body.

Lucas looms behind me, stepping so close, I can feel his shirt against my back. He makes a sudden flash movement, and before I can register what he's doing, he grips the back of my neck in his hand and forces my head down.

"I said play with her fucking tits. Bite them." His words are deadly, dark, cold.

His dominance completely consumes him. And I let it. I give into his desires.

My eyes glance up from below my lashes toward Tia. She licks her lips in response to us, and her chest heaves slightly. She's turned on. I snap the straps of her dress in my palms, setting her tits free.

Tia throws her head back in pleasure the moment my teeth graze her flesh. I nip and suck while she moans and holds my head in place, and Lucas holds my neck. His rough, tight grip bites into my pulse points, sending a sick need to punish Tia through me. I slam into her harder, sending her head flying back and hitting the wall.

"Oh god, Cole. I'm going to . . ."

"Come, Tia. Come on his cock. Milk his cock for him like a good girl."

His words and Tia's viselike grip on my cock send my orgasm spiraling. As if sensing my release, Lucas grips me tighter. "Suck."

One word, and I explode, flooding her pussy and sending drips down my balls. I stumble forward, pushing her harder into the wall.

Her orgasm milks my cock dry.

He releases my neck, and I stand tall once again. My eyes take a moment to refocus, but I'm automatically aware he's no longer there. The moment his fingers left me, I knew he'd be gone, like he was never here to begin with.

"Is he okay?" Tia stares down the corridor, and when his door slams shut, it makes her jump. Tears fill her eyes, and I want to strangle the prick for hurting her. For hurting me too.

I gently kiss her lips.

"He's gone to bash one out," I joke, trying to lighten the mood.

She gives me a sad smile that I want to erase forever.

I swallow harshly, overcome with the emotions of the night. "I love you."

Now her smile broadens into a genuine one, one that makes my chest swell like I'm the best motherfucker in the world.

"I love you, too."

CHAPTER
EIGHTEEN

Tia

Moaning and whimpers stir me from my sleep, and I jolt with the realization that it's Lucas. I scramble with the sheets, grateful I have on my sleep shorts and camisole. Glancing back at Cole, his lips part on a gentle snore. He lies exposed with his cock at half-mast, his arm behind his head, and his huge chest begging for me to lick him, but another wail causes my stomach to flip and my feet to move toward the door.

Lucas only sleeps next door. I give his open door a gentle knock and enter. Straight away, his cologne hits me, taunts me, drawing me in further.

He's fighting in his bed, tangled in his sheets. His ripped body strains with pain. His face is contorted, and a coat of sweat mars his olive skin.

"Lucas." I use a low voice as I approach his bed, conscious not to scare him further. "Lucas. Wake up."

"Please. Don't hurt me. I'm sorry. Please," he whimpers into the pillow before he lets out a low moan of pain. "Ahhh."

My heart jackknifes at his harrowing whimpers, pleading with someone not to hurt him.

"Please, stop."

I crawl over the bed. "Lucas. Wake up."

"Ahh." His body spasms and freezes. "Please."

I lean over him, this being the closest I've ever come to touching him. "Lucas?" I graze my hand over his face, trailing it gently over his clammy skin. His hand snaps onto my wrist from nowhere, and his eyes flare open. He throws me onto my back and mounts me so fast I don't have time to speak.

A sharp prick digs into my flesh just below my face, and a few seconds later, I register he has a knife pressed under my chin.

His eyes are dark and despondent, like he's not even seeing me at all. My throat dries in fear as he stares down at me with complete loathing in his eyes.

"Lu—" I struggle to swallow. "Lucas. It's me, Tia." I stroke my hand up his arm that's caging me in.

In a split second, he seems to snap out of his trance but makes no motion to move. His eyes soften slightly, but the knife stays in place with my chin raised high.

"What are you doing in my room?"

"You . . . you were crying out in your sleep. I wanted to make sure you were okay."

"Why?"

"Because I care about you."

He scoffs. "You care about me?"

"I see you, Lucas." I wet my suddenly dry lips as I go

on to explain. "We share something. A connection maybe?"

Lucas stares at me, not confirming or denying my analysis.

He shakes his head. "You don't see the darkness in me, Tia."

I tilt my head slightly, and his grip allows it. "I see it, and I match it, Lucas." My eyes bore into his. "We're drowning in it. But maybe . . ." I swallow hard, and his body tenses above me. ". . . maybe we can drown in our darkness together."

His grip on the knife tightens, forcing me to freeze.

"I could kill you if I wanted to. Watch the blood pour from your pretty little face."

His face is so close I can feel the heat from his breath, and my skin breaks out with tingles of awareness. He's trying to scare me away, but I refuse to give in.

"You think I'm pretty?" I smirk, raising my chin further.

Lucas loosens the pinch of the knife ever so slightly. "You know I do." His eyes plead with love, and the realization makes my heart skip a beat. He presses his body down slightly on mine, and I can feel his hardness against me. Wetness pools between my legs in response.

"Lucas." I pant in need.

"I . . . I can't." His face is laced in disappointment, and my mind races to come to a solution for him. He wants to give in, but his mind won't allow it. Whatever demons Lucas has, they're controlling him, letting him be a shadow of a man he's capable of becoming.

His hand shakes, but the knife stays just below my

chin as his security. He can touch me—be close to me—because he has his knife. It allows him the small comfort in order for him to go as far as this.

"Cut me."

Lucas's eyebrows draw together in confusion.

"Use your knife and cut me, Lucas. I know you want to." I force my hips up toward his erection, rubbing myself on him. His face transforms on a groan at the connection, and I swear it's the most erotic sound I've ever heard.

A sharp pinch makes my eyes flare. His soft wet tongue licks away the wound and pushes his hips against mine with a moan, my own moan following behind his.

His knife nicks me again on my chin, and this time, his gentle mouth sucks at the tender flesh, his reaction a complete contrast to the action.

He pulls back and scans my face, his nostrils flaring as he gazes down at our bodies before he glances back up at me and draws me in with his face full of uncertainty. "I don't know what to do, Tia." My eyebrows furrow, unsure of what exactly he means. "I . . . I don't know how to please you."

My shoulders relax slightly on his admittance, and I ease into the mattress when he moves the knife beside us but still tight in his grasp.

"Can you touch me?" My tongue glides over my lip, his intensity penetrating my skin, my own barriers and insecurities. I've gone from not wanting a relationship at all to wanting two men.

"I don't know how." He gazes down my body, the

feeling of his perusal electrifying. His shoulders are bunched tight, and his muscles flex, as though he's holding himself back.

"Touch me." I pant needily.

His hand trembles as it moves lightly over my chest, down and over my stomach so lightly, I barely know he's touching me at all. He dips his fingers into the waistband of my sleep shorts, and I suck in a sharp breath and refrain from bucking into him eagerly. I want to give him time to explore on his own.

His fingers connect with the top of my pussy, and wetness seeps from me. He brushes over my clit, and my body coils tightly beneath him as he slips between my folds and down to my hole.

"Is this okay?" His tender words melt me both inside and out.

"Yes." I breathe out through tight lips, desperate to scream for more.

He presses a finger inside me. "Oh fuck. You're wet." He withdraws, then pushes back in again, repeating the motion over and over.

I choke on a laugh. "I am."

"You can hold on to me if you want." His gray, stormy eyes find mine, and I smile in delight at him pushing his boundaries for me.

I take hold of his shoulders, his skin soft and smooth beneath my touch. I trail my palms over his skin as he begins to pump his finger in and out of my pussy before he withdraws and adds another.

"You feel so good, Tia." I clench my pussy around his fingers. "Fuck, do that again." I do as he instructs.

"Fuck." Lucas bites the inside of his mouth as though struggling to control himself. His thumb breezes over my clit, making my pussy ache to be filled.

"Oh god." His eyes flick up to mine in concern. "It's okay. Don't stop." I buck up into him, and he presses his thumb down harder, circling my clit.

"I'm going to come, Lucas."

"Oh fuck. Come on my fingers, Tia. Let me feel you." His hips buck against mine, pushing his fingers further inside me while his thumb presses down, igniting an explosion from deep inside me.

"Lucas! Fuck, fuck!" I scream out his name while he watches me in awe as I come on his fingers like he instructed.

"Such a good girl." He peppers tender kisses down my neck. "Such a good girl, coating my fingers with your cum."

I pant heavily against him. "Please. I need to please you, Lucas."

Lucas pulls back sharply, removing his fingers from my shorts. He drags a ragged hand through his already messy hair, and I sit up on my elbows with concern that he's retreating.

"It's okay. I'm sorry." I nibble my lip, not knowing what to say or do. I've pushed him too far, and the thought hits me in my stomach like a lead weight.

Lucas stares at me, sitting back on his haunches, his thick erection protruding through his boxer shorts tauntingly.

"Can you . . . Can just touch me or something?" he asks.

My pulse races, and my body relaxes as I give him a small nod. "Of course. Whatever you want."

His pupils darken, and he moves to the end of the bed. Glancing nervously around the room, he slides down his boxer shorts without looking at me. His cock springs out with pre-cum oozing from the tip.

He moves to lie beside me with his head on the pillow. I take him in, scanning his perfectly sculpted body from head to toe. His thick cock almost touches his belly button. It's smooth with a protruding vein I want to trail my tongue along.

Lucas takes hold of the knife; his grip on it sends his knuckles white. I trail my fingers down his face as he watches on, transfixed by my movement. My hand glides over the smooth planes of his abs, and his breath quickens. I sit up on the bed, staring down at him laid out for me. My hand breezes over his stomach and down toward his cock, making it jump.

"Tell me if you want me to stop," I urge him with sincerity.

"Don't." His eyes latch on to mine, trusting and vulnerable, needy and determined.

The air around us is thick and filled with desire. Want.

My hands circle his thick, smooth cock.

"Fuck." His lips part in shock, and his Adam's apple bobs in wonder. He chokes slightly. "Fuck. That's good. Don't stop."

His chest heaves rapidly, and the heat from his body permeates from him. I work his cock up and down in a tight fist and move my free hand to his balls. As soon as my hand touches them, he arches into my touch with a hiss. "Holy shit, Tia."

The look of complete ecstasy on his face makes my pussy throb with need. He's gorgeous. Absolutely gorgeous. I feel like he's giving me a gift. Giving me something he refuses to share with others.

"Lucas," I breathe out his name for no reason other than to appreciate it on my tongue, to marvel in the knowledge that it's me who has control over his release.

"Fuck." He bucks up into my hand, and I tighten my grip on him. I slide my hand up and down, occasionally grazing the pulsating head. It's saturated in pre-cum and looks ready to blow at any second. "Oh fuck. It's coming."

His lips part, and his eyes widen as ropes of thick cum hit us. His stomach is covered, and my hand is dripping in his warmth. His gaze is resting on my hand as his cock begins to deflate.

"Shit. I should clean up." He jumps up from the bed and rushes toward the bathroom before coming back with a warm washcloth. I watch him in confusion. "Give me your hand, Tia."

I hold out my hand while he gently washes away his cum. Disappointment fills my stomach at the feeling that he's washing away what he's just done, what he's achieved.

"What's wrong?"

I glance away, unable to convey my feelings. He takes my chin in his forefingers and lifts my head to face him.

"I like you on me," I admit weakly.

His lips turn up in a confident smirk. "That so?" I

nod. "Rub it in, then. Make sure you smell of me, baby girl."

Wetness pools between my thighs, leaving my sleep shorts sticky at the use of the new nickname for me. My eyes flare in delight, unable to conceal my arousal. Lucas's pupils dilate, and his tongue grazes over his lips before he takes a step back and glances away, breaking the moment between us.

I don't want to push him, not when he's just opening up to me. To us.

He throws the cloth into the laundry bin, tugs on his boxers, and climbs into bed beside me. I pull the sheets up and lie on my side, facing him, unsure of whether to rest on him or simply touch him.

Lucas clears his throat. "You can lay your head on my chest if you want?" He turns his eyes toward me, a glimmer of uncertainty shining through them.

I shuffle forward and place my hand on his chest while resting my head over his thundering heart. He lies stoically still, almost frozen below me, before he picks up my hand and gently kisses it.

"I've wanted to touch you for so long. Longer than you can imagine."

His words breeze over my head tenderly. I've only been here just over a week, so I find that hard to believe, but still, the notion of him wanting me so greatly wraps around my heart like a warm blanket.

"For so long," he whispers as he strokes his fingers lovingly through my hair until my eyes feel heavy and my heart full.

NINETEEN

C ole

Opening my brother's bedroom door wider, I take in the sight of my girlfriend sprawled out over Lucas's chest. Love seeps from me. Two of the people I love most in the world are together, and I yearn to join them. But I won't, not yet.

As if sensing me, Tia's eyes open and automatically find mine. They flare in panic, and I want nothing more than to reassure her.

I creep toward her and kneel beside the bed as she rolls over to face me. The guilt coating her face assaults me, and I hate it, not when whatever she did was to reassure my brother. Help him. I can't deny the milestone. This is for Lucas. They have a connection only they can understand, and I won't stand in their way of supporting one another through their pain. Because I love them. Both of them.

I gently tuck a loose curl behind her ear. "It's okay,

beauty." My lips meet hers, and I revel in the whimper that escapes her lips. I glance toward a sleeping Lucas. "Thank you for giving him comfort."

Her eyes dart over my face, frantically causing me to shake my head. "I don't care, Tia. I want you. Both of you, beauty."

Her shoulders relax, and her lips turn up into a sweet smile.

"You can fuck my brother, I'm good with that." I leave my words hanging there.

How I want Lucas, I'm not really sure, but right now, as I stand and walk toward the open door, I know my love for my brother is much more than familial.

I just hope he feels the same way.

I OPEN the door to my brother's office and glance back toward Tia, who's sitting at the dining table studying. Then, I step inside.

Closing the door behind me with a soft click, Lucas's eyes find mine as he peers over the paperwork he's working through.

"Did you fuck her?" My tone comes out clipped.

His eyes stay locked on mine. "No." My shoulders relax, hearing the sincerity in his voice. Lucas searches my face. "Would it bother you if I did?"

My heart hammers, and I move from foot to foot. Would it bother me? It should. But the thought of my brother finally giving in and building a relationship with the one woman I love doesn't fill me with jealousy or anger. It fills me with intrigue and pride for them loving one another, and it also fills my cock with a need to be fulfilled to experience them together. See it with my own eyes.

It's fucked up. I know it's fucked up, but I want that. I want them both.

"No. It doesn't bother me." I stare at him, unblinking.

His body relaxes at my words. "We didn't have sex." He glances away as though suddenly embarrassed. This is new for Lucas, and as much as he likes to play the voyeur and dominant, something tells me, in reality, he's going to struggle to fulfill that side of himself.

At least he has me and Tia to help him achieve it.

"I'm not sure I can do it."

My heart aches for him with his admittance; the broken edge in his voice leaves me eager to help him.

I step forward. "She'll help you, man. I'll help you." My eyes drill into him, forcing him to turn his face toward me.

"I don't want you to hate me."

There's a quiver behind his words that makes me frown in confusion. What isn't he telling me?

I go for lightening the mood. "Well, if you think you can steal her from under me, good luck with that. Our girl loves my pierced cock too much." I stroke along the line of my cock in my jeans, pushing my chest out when Lucas's pupils dilate. I'm not even sure he's aware I can see the lust behind his eyes, and not for the first time, my cock twitches at the thought of him liking me like that.

I've never had any experience with guys, never felt a connection toward them either. But Lucas? Lucas is different, and I know he can feel the connection too.

The chances of him acting on it are very slim, not with the trauma he suffers from.

"I have a surprise for Tia tomorrow," he says.

I snap out of my thoughts. "Yeah?"

"She can have Harper for the day."

This piques my interest as I move closer to his desk. "Go on . . ."

"Our lawyer argued for more time, and we got it."

My eyebrows shoot up in surprise. "I thought it was going to take a while."

Lucas nods. "Let's just say Mr. Lancaster enjoys fucking his interns, so he was happy to negotiate."

I chuckle at Lucas's tactics and cross my arms over my chest. "So, what shall we do tomorrow?"

"We?" His eyebrows furrow.

I roll my eyes at his nonchalance. "Us. You think we're going without you when we have only just had you?" I joke.

"No, of course not." He stammers and drags a hand through his hair. "It's just I didn't think . . . I didn't think . . . I'd . . ." His Adam's apple bobs, forcing me to take pity on him.

"You didn't think you'd be invited?"

He nods. "Yeah."

I laugh sarcastically. "If you're going to be fucking her mom, I think you need to meet her. Besides, Tia would want you there." I shrug.

As I turn and walk toward the door, he stops me in my tracks. "I'm not sure I'll be fucking her mom."

I turn my head over my shoulder. "You will." I wink.

Damn fucking right he will.

When Lucas gives in to his deepest desires, it's going to be one big dirty fuck fest, and I cannot wait.

TIA

My mind has been in overdrive all day. I've struggled to concentrate on anything other than Lucas and his inability to give in. I want him. I want him so fucking bad it hurts—both my heart and my pussy—because all day long, the dull throb between my legs hasn't been dealt with. God, do I feel needy.

Cole left this morning to train some fighters at his gym, then tonight, he's going to be home late because there's a fight scheduled. Apparently, Rage would normally take over at night because the guy doesn't sleep, but he's away on some business trip.

Lucas had explained at breakfast that they're planning on buying a bunch of nightclubs on the West Coast, so Rage has gone over in advance of the meetings to check them out as a customer before sitting down to start negotiations.

Lucas has been in his office all day, and I get the feeling he's avoiding me. I take another glance at his door, wondering when he'll eventually come out. If he'll come out.

Maybe I should take him a drink or something?

I bite on my lip before breathing out and pushing away from the table. I take a beer out of the refrigerator, flick the cap on the bottle, and make my way toward his office.

Should I knock on his door? I raise my fist to place a gentle knock against the wood before pushing open the door.

Lucas's gray eyes shoot up from his computer. They lock me into a stare, and my feet are suddenly frozen, unsure of entering in the first place.

"I brought you a beer." My hand nervously finds my neck, playing with the necklace clasped around it. I toy with it between my fingers.

"Thank you."

He holds his hand out for the beer, so I step closer and hold the beer out for him. Just as his fingers graze the bottle, he tugs on the seam of my dress and pulls me closer so I'm standing between his widened legs. He strokes the fabric of my dress with his fingers, each movement sensual somehow.

My chest flushes when his hand creeps to the inside of my thigh, and my pulse races and my clit throbs when his light touch moves farther up my dress. Lucas doesn't look away from me; he stares into my eyes as though daring me to move, but I stand frozen, allowing him the time to explore. All the while, my breathing escalates, making it harder for me to act unfazed.

"Are you wearing panties?"

"Yes," I choke out needily.

He tsks. "Don't. Don't wear them in the apartment anymore." His gray eyes drill into mine with no room for disagreement. "If I want to finger your pussy and play with your clit, I want access to it at all times." His words send a surge of arousal through my body, and I squeeze my thighs in response.

"You like me talking dirty to you?"

I nod and move my hand toward his shoulder but then stop, unsure of his reaction to me.

"Do you want me to tell you what filthy thoughts I'm having right now, Tia?"

"Y-Yes."

Lucas smirks. In such a way, it's erotic. It makes me want to slap him, lick him better, then ride his handsome face.

"Is your pussy wet?" His nostrils flare, and his tongue darts out to wet his lips. The action makes me whimper needily.

"Yes."

"Take your panties off, Tia. Sit on the desk, and let me see your dripping cunt."

I move quickly, pulling my panties down my legs and kicking them beside his desk. I pull myself onto his desk, placing both my shaky feet onto the wood. Then, I open my legs wide for him. He moves his chair to position himself closer to me.

Slowly, he takes a pull of his beer. All the while, his eyes stay locked on mine, before ducking down toward my open legs.

He sucks in a sharp breath. "Fuck. Open yourself up for me."

I lean up on my elbows and use both hands to open my slick folds for him to see me exposed before him.

Lucas moves the beer bottle, dragging the top of the bottle lazily down my pussy. The coldness of the glass makes my skin break out in goose bumps and my body to involuntarily shake beneath its touch.

A groan leaves his lips, and my heart races at the sound.

He repeats the action, forcing my body to tense up, before he pushes the open bottle into my pussy—only slightly—before gazing up at me as though checking I'm okay with this. Being fucked by an open bottle.

He pushes in further, the cool glass sinking inside me. "Fuck, that's hot." His eyes are transfixed on the bottle, wide-eyed in awe. "Fuck yourself on the bottle and play with your clit. Get off for me."

I swallow deeply, suddenly unsure of how I feel, so open and exposed with a foreign object thrust inside me.

"Now," his sharp voice commands.

I move my finger and begin circling my clit. "Ahhh."

He pushes the bottle further inside, before he withdraws and repeats the motion. I'm now so wet, it glides in with ease. My pussy tries to grip it, but I don't have time before he withdraws, then repeats the motion again.

"Oh god, Lucas." I add an extra finger to my clit and press down harder, swirling faster when the cold bottle is thrust inside me harder.

"Such a dirty little slut, being fucked by a bottle." His darkened tone adds to my arousal.

"More," I beg wantonly.

He thrusts in harder, the force making me lift my ass off the desk. "You're taking it so good."

The praise behind his words sends a gush of wetness around the rim, and heat breaks out over my entire body.

"Fuck. Such a slut. You love taking that bottle for me. Letting me shove a bottle in your tight cunt. Such a good girl."

I melt at his words. My pussy clenches harder around the bottle. "Oh god, Lucas."

"That's it, say my name while I fuck you with a bottle. Be a good girl and come inside it. Let me drink you down. Let me savor every." *Thrust.* "Fucking." *Thrust.* "Mouthful." *Thrust.* "Of your pussy juice."

I throw my head back against the desk as my body tightens around the glass. "Yes, oh god."

I come. I come so hard I see lights behind my eyes. My ears throb with the loud beating of my heart.

He withdraws the bottle.

Slowly, I come down from my orgasm and lift my head. Lucas's stare is trained on me, his mouth open in ecstasy and his hand tight around the bottle.

"Get on your knees," he chokes out.

I scramble to the floor as he stands and unbuckles his belt. I watch as he takes his thick cock in his hand, the head angry and coated with pre-cum. He pumps it.

"Open your mouth and stick your tongue out. Don't swallow."

My eyes flare at his words. I stare at him as he pumps

his cock roughly with one hand, his eyes drilling into mine and his nostrils flaring, making his actions appear wild. He takes a drink of the bottle, and his eyes close in delight as though savoring the flavor.

"Fucking perfect," he mumbles. "Fuck." His hips work, thrusting forward into his tight fist. "Fuck. You belong to me. My slut to play with, baby girl. Mine." He stares down at me wildly. "Fuck."

He comes. The head of his cock squirts hot, thick cum deliberately over my face, before he aims it into my open mouth, coating my tongue and making me moan in pleasure.

His orgasm fades, taking with it the animalistic look about him.

Lucas drinks the rest of the beer before slamming the bottle onto the table and turning back toward me. "Swallow, baby girl."

I do as he asks and swallow his cum. He watches me closely, and a look of pride crosses over his face.

"Such a perfect girl for me to play with." His words hit deep in my heart, causing it to skip a beat. They echo in my mind. "For me to play with." Is that all I am to him? A toy to play with? Am I some sort of experiment to him? So that he can find the confidence, then move on? Hurt swirls inside me, and suddenly, I want to run. I want to get as far away from Lucas as I possibly can.

"What did I say?" Lucas stares at me in confusion, clearly picking up on the change in me.

"What am I to you, Lucas?" I stand and cross my arms over my chest, feeling vulnerable with his cum still on my face. Like a dirty fuck toy. I wince at the thought.

He stares at me, as though he's unsure about my outburst. Slowly, like I'm a wounded animal, he tucks a loose strand of hair behind my ear. "You're our everything." It isn't lost on me that he said "our."

"I need you to promise me something, Tia." He bends and rests his forehead against mine. "I need you to know that everything I do, it's for us. All of us." I nod at his words, but I'm unclear what he means. "I'd do anything to protect you."

The blood pulsates through my body. There's a hidden meaning behind his words, yet they're clear, nonetheless.

"I understand," I utter back to him, but I'm still unsure what I'm understanding. Only that he's going to protect me. Protect us both. And what more could I possibly ask?

Lucas slowly drags his tongue over my cheek, lapping up the remains of his cum. "Our beautiful fuck toy, baby girl." This time his words warm me.

Wrapped in brutal hidden devotion.

CHAPTER TWENTY

C ole
Harper holds my hand while bouncing on
the balls of her feet. "She's here, can you see?"
I point toward the car Lucas just pulled up in.

When he told me to collect Harper this morning from
the Lancasters' and text him somewhere to meet that
was child friendly, I knew this was not what he had in
mind.

I can feel his glare before he even steps foot out of the
car, making me chuckle to myself.

"Mommy!" Harper screeches, then slips from my
hand to run toward Tia. Tia's face morphs from shock to
sheer delight, and I steal a glance at Lucas, hoping he
realizes what he's done for Tia. For both of them. His
normally stoic face turns up with a small smile as he
watches on. Tia hugs Harper in a tight embrace.

"How did this happen?" She looks between me and
Lucas.

"He did it." I throw my arm out toward Lucas. He nervously drags a hand through his dark hair.

Tia jumps to her feet and plants a kiss on his cheek before he has a chance to pull away. I narrow my eyes when he doesn't shy away from her. Mmm, interesting. What's been happening while I've been working these crazy-ass shifts? And when the fuck is Rage home so I can see?

"When is Rage home?"

Lucas turns toward me, his glare bordering on deadly. "Another week."

Shit, he's been gone a long time for him. He'll be raging at Lucas when he gets home, that's for sure. I chuckle to myself at my own analogy. Poor dude is going to lose his shit when he realizes not only he has a woman living with him, but his brothers are sharing her and she has a kid I'm quite happy to take on as my own.

I gaze at my family before me. Fucking perfect. Tia introduces Lucas to Harper, and like the little superstar she is, she latches onto his hand and her mom's, and they start walking toward the beach.

Lucas stops at my ear. "The fucking beach?" He glances down at his business clothes, shirt, and slacks in disgust.

I shrug with a grin. "I bought you some swimmers." I hold up the bag from the nearby surf shop. "I got Harper some too. Woman in the shop said you can change in there." I nod toward the store.

"Thank you, Cole. I love you." Harper throws her arms around my legs, and I grin widely at Lucas.

"She loves me." I raise my eyebrows and wiggle them.

Lucas stares down at Harper, then back up at me. "Game-fucking-on, brother." His sly grin makes me throw my head back on a laugh.

LUCAS APPROACHES in a small pair of black swim shorts; his toned olive body has the perfect number of ridges. He's nowhere near as built or as wide as me, but he is ripped. I glance down toward his impressive bulge. I've never taken proper notice of this, but now the thought of seeing him naked for me and Tia makes my cock jerk.

It's completely unlike him to be so naked. If it wasn't for his clenched jaw and coiled shoulder muscles, you wouldn't know he's uncomfortable. To the outside world, he looks pissed, but to me, he's trying to disguise his discomfort.

I glance at Tia. She's smiling up at him, as though he's a hero for arranging this. She's so damn beautiful, and for a moment, I feel like the air is being sucked from my chest. I'm going to marry this girl. Someday. Someday, she's going to be my wife, and her adorable little girl is going to be mine too. I'll make sure of it.

I can't help but laugh when Lucas almost wipes a whole family out with the giant inflatable princess carriage and then stumbles due to the amount of sand toys he's laden with.

He drops them at my feet with a huff, making me smile up at him in amusement. "Couldn't you decide between the pink unicorn or the purple one?" I ask, pointing toward the virtually identical buckets.

He narrows his eyes at me before kicking sand over my freshly sun-creamed abs.

"Lucas, that's not nice. You don't kick sand, it can be dangerous," Harper reprimands Lucas with her cute nose scrunching up and her hands on her hips. "Mommy, tell Lucas to be a good boy." She wags her finger in Lucas's direction, earning a low chuckle from him. It's clear he's struggling to keep a straight face, so he bites into his lip.

"Be a good boy, Lucas."

"Yeah, Lucas. Be a good boy," I mock. He rewards me with the middle finger as Harper bends down to unpack the abundance of sand toys.

"This is incredible, guys. Thank you both so much." Tears fill Tia's eyes, and I feel the immediate need to comfort her, but Lucas beats me to it. He places a tender arm around her waist, drawing her into him. Then, she rests her head on his chest like it's the most normal thing in the world.

To anyone else, it would be, but to Lucas, it isn't. I scan his body, looking for discomfort, but the only tell-tale is his toes curling into the sand.

"Lucas. Can you help build a princess castle?"

His eyes snap down toward Harper, who's sitting in the sand already digging a hole. A smile tugs on his usually grumpy lips, and he lowers himself to the ground to help her. "Sure." He gifts her with a smile I've never seen before, and she mirrors one back at him. The exchange between the two makes my heart swell.

"Hey, what about me? What shall I do?"

"You can go fetch the water, Cole. You have giant arms for that." She waves the spade around in her hand, pointing toward my arms, sending sand flying without even realizing. She's so damn cute.

Tia lowers herself to sit beside me. "And a giant cock too." Her words breeze into my ear.

"Jesus, beauty. Don't say shit like that to me while we're here." I nod toward Harper, causing Tia to stifle a giggle. "I'm going to get water for our princess." I jump up before my cock has other ideas. No way do I want to be called out for that shit happening on a family beach.

Later, though, later it can be up all night long.

I'm going to make her pay.

Her and Lucas.

TIA

Harper pours another bucket of sand on top of Cole. You can only see his head now, and he's grinning from ear to ear, seemingly loving it as much as Harper, if not more—if that's even possible.

Her giggle seems to travel in the sea breeze. "You're covered now, mister sand man."

"I am. You're right. How do I go to the bathroom?" he asks in mock horror.

She bends down toward his ear. "Cole, do you need to pee?"

Cole looks at me, as though I know whether he needs to pee or not. "No, I'm good."

"Okay, cos big boys hold their pee."

Cole nods at her in agreement.

"Lucas, can you save some of those shells for me?" Harper asks. "I like the pretty ones that shine."

Lucas holds a shell up to show Harper. "Like this one?"

"Yep."

"Okay, I'll pop it in the pink bucket."

"You know what I need?" We turn our heads toward Cole.

"Do you need to pee?" Harper asks with a raised eyebrow.

"No, I need an ice cream."

Harper's eyebrows shoot up, and she glances toward me in question.

"I got them." Lucas stands and brushes the sand from his legs. "Are you coming to choose, Harper?"

"Can I, Mommy?" Her blue eyes meet mine, and not for the first time today, I consider how much my little girl is like me. And not like him.

"Sure." I smile tightly like I always do when thoughts of him invade me.

Lucas takes Harper's hand, and they walk toward the ice cream store.

"Beauty, can you help me out of here?" Cole tilts his head toward the sand, making me chuckle that his head is poking out of the top.

I lean over Cole and breeze my lips over his in a sly movement that doesn't quite equate to a kiss. "I think I like you restrained."

"Beauty, the only restraining going on will be when you're tied to my bed later." He moves his face forward, taking my lips in his. He pushes his tongue into my mouth, and I moan at the sensation of his piercing flicking inside.

"Fuck, beauty, I'm so damn hard, my cock could drill through the sand."

I pull back laughing. "Now that would be funny!"

"Yeah?" He smirks. Then, he rests his head down before making me jump when he forces his body up from the sand with an almighty roar and lunges for me. Throwing me over his sand-covered shoulder, he slaps my ass cheek and runs toward the water, throwing us both into the waves.

He lowers me down his body, and I wrap my hands around his neck.

"I love you, beauty." His green eyes sparkle with love and admiration.

"I love you too."

His lips meet mine. Every grain of sand is washed away, along with every doubt in my mind that the three of us were never meant to be.

CHAPTER
TWENTY-ONE

T ia

I stare at the open door to our bedroom. Cole is snoozing beside me, but I can't sleep, even after him fucking me twice and me coming so many times. I even struggled to remember my own name. My mind wanders to Lucas and why he didn't join us. Why he didn't stand in the shadows.

He went to his room to shower, and we haven't seen him since.

I sigh, my body deflating with the thought of him being alone and feeling unwelcome.

"Go to him, beauty," Cole mumbles from beside me, as if sensing my inner turmoil.

I glance back at him, a soft smile playing on his lips, but his eyes are closed, making me wonder if he's dreaming.

"Go," he mumbles again.

I throw the sheet off me and make my way toward his room.

Stepping inside his bedroom, I'm surprised to find Lucas awake in bed and staring straight at me, making me startle. Without saying a word, he throws open the covers for me to climb in, so I waste no time in joining him.

"I miss her, Lucas."

He pulls me toward him. "Tia, I'm going to get her back for you. I promise."

The truth seeps from his eyes, and hope blossoms inside me. I've never felt as confident as I do now in the fight toward getting my little girl back where she belongs.

"I couldn't sleep," I admit softly while resting my head on his chest.

"Me too." His fingers find my hair, soothing me. "I had a nightmare."

"I'm sorry."

He scoffs. "It's not your fault." His heart races. "I didn't have one the night you stayed in here." His words shouldn't comfort me, because it's fucked up that he has to deal with that, but they do. He needs me as much as I need him.

"You could join us." I glance up at him.

"I can't have sex, Tia. I'm fucking broken." He snipes the words out, then winces, as though realizing his tone.

"Have you . . . have you never done it before?" I cringe at my wording. My body fills with trepidation, waiting for his response.

"Not willingly. No."

A sharp pain hits me in the chest, and my blood boils around his body. I knew he had demons, knew he had trauma, but there was a part of me that hoped—prayed—it wasn't this.

"You understand." He repeats the same words as I once told him. And I know without a shadow of a doubt that he knows my history. My body tightens at the thought.

Did Cole tell him?

"I think sometimes we can see it in one another, you know? Like there's a light there in your eyes, and I can see the pain. Because the same pain is the one I see reflecting back at me in the mirror every morning."

My muscles loosen. Maybe Cole didn't tell.

"You can't let them win, Lucas. You've so much to give." My hand plays lightly over his chest, his warmth traveling from the tips of my fingers into my heart.

"I'm not sure how." He swallows.

"By being yourself. You like orchestrating things between me and Cole." He nods against me, so I carry on. "You could do those things too. I want you to. We want you to."

"I'm not gay." He spits the words out unexpectedly, making me raise my head from his chest to stare at him.

"Why would you say that?"

"I'm just saying that I'm not."

"Did someone call you that?" I search his face for a sign. Of what, I'm not sure.

"My . . . my father was the one who did things to me."

I close my eyes in understanding. His father abused him.

"We had sex."

I open my eyes to find him staring at me, waiting for

195

a reaction.

"You were raped, Lucas. That's not sex. There's a difference."

"I know that," he snaps once again. Then, he drags his hand aggressively through his hair in annoyance with himself. He exhales loudly. "It's just . . . sometimes, I think about it."

I turn my head up toward him. "In what way?"

"In ways that make me feel sick about myself for even thinking it."

"You can talk to me, Lucas." I glide my hand down the side of his face in a comforting gesture.

His Adam's apple bobs. "Some of the things I was forced to do . . ." He squeezes his eyes shut. ". . . I want to try them now."

His heart hammers below me and his body is stiff, indicating how much he's struggling with the situation.

I keep my tone low and soothing. "Whatever you were forced to do when you were a child, Lucas, was out of your hands. You. Were. Forced. You shouldn't feel shame in wanting to experiment or experience things, Lucas. You're an adult, and you're in control now."

"I need to be in control." His voice darkens and is laced with an undertone of certainty, leaving no room for negotiation. Whatever situation we're going to be in, Lucas will always need to be in control. There is no other option.

His arm tightens around me, both lovingly and protectively. I snuggle down into him. "Besides, I like when you control situations." I smile into his chest, and he rewards me with a gentle kiss to my head.

I STARE at Cole in disbelief as he throws punch after punch to his opponent's stomach, following it up with a swift kick to his chest. The strength behind his assault soaks my panties and causes my thighs to clench in anticipation for his match to finish.

Sweat pours from him, and his muscles pull tight with each action. The crowd goes wild, but all I can really hear is the beating of my heart willing this match to end.

As the referee rings the bell to announce the end of the round, I leap to my feet and rush toward him.

Cole smirks in my direction, as though knowing I wouldn't miss out on being there for him. He ignores the trainer who talks in his ear and instead pushes his head through the ropes and takes me by my neck, pulling me in for a kiss that consumes me. I moan into his mouth, and he responds by flicking his tongue over mine, knowing the ball of his piercing drives me wild.

He pulls back, panting. "Fuck, beauty. I'm going to have to fight with a semi."

I glance down toward his shorts, and sure enough, his cock is standing at half-mast. I swear, I can see his piercing rubbing against his shorts, trying to get out of his tight constraints, and I want nothing more than to drop to my knees and help relieve him.

His trainer tugs him away, and he mouths a *love you* toward me, making me smile in delight. As much as I've enjoyed watching Cole, I cannot wait for this fight to end so that I can reward him.

"Come and sit down. You look like you're about to

drop to your knees in front of everyone." Lucas smirks into my ear, and I do as he asks, planting my ass firmly on the chair in front of the ring.

Cole takes a punch to his face, and I wince, but he barely flinches. Lucas's hand finds my thigh, and he gives it a reassuring squeeze.

"It's okay, baby girl." His fingers tease the hem of my dress. "Daddy's here."

I suck in a sharp breath at his words, but I jolt when Cole takes another blow to his stomach. His eyes dart toward Lucas's hand, and I realize he's being distracted, so I push Lucas's hand away abruptly, causing him to chuckle. Instead, he opts to stretch his arm over the back of my chair and rests his hand on my shoulder.

Cole's opponent has noticed his distraction, and I watch as he mouths something to Cole. Whatever reaction the idiot thought he was going to get isn't the one he receives, because Cole unleashes hell on him. Slamming his fists repeatedly into the jerk's side, he makes a quick move to jump into the air, following it up with a fancy kick that makes my eyes bug out and the guy slam to the floor when Cole's foot connects with his face.

The referee rings the bell and grips a hold of Cole's wrist, raising it into the air.

"He won?" I question Lucas.

"He did," he drawls lazily as though unfazed.

"Yes!" I jump to my feet, jumping up and down in delight, and when Cole's eyes lock with mine, a heat breaks out over my skin, and I know his assault on my body is going to be so much more rewarding.

COLE

I glance at Tia again. Tonight, she came to my match and saw me fight. I was fucking hard the whole fight, knowing her eyes were trained on me. Her cheers were for me.

When I unleashed a killer roundhouse kick to my opponent, and he went down, she flew so quickly from her chair toward the cage that her tits almost fell out of her damn dress.

Lucas quickly came to her rescue, encouraging her to sit back down. As he placed his hand on her knee, my cock twitched at the thought of him parting her legs for me.

I almost ran to the changing room for a quick shower and change so we could get the hell out of there.

"Cole. Are you listening?"

Soft hands touch my face and gently steer my face toward Tia. "I said, can we dance?"

"You did?"

Her eyebrows shoot up, and she laughs to herself. "You were in your own little world there. Care to share?"

Damn fucking right I want to share.

I take a pull of my beer and smirk at Lucas as he narrows his eyes at me. "I'm good with sharing." I grin.

Tia rolls her eyes. "Come on. Come share me on the dance floor." She stands tall in her red fuck-me heels and a flimsy red dress she most definitely shouldn't be wearing in this club. I can tell Lucas is ready to pull that knife of his out and take pricks' eyes out for daring to look at our girl.

She tugs at both of our hands, and like the saps we are, we follow her toward the dance floor.

I spin her to face me, while Lucas's hands find her hips. Tia drapes her arms over my neck, and I tug her closer to me. My hands land on her thighs, inching her dress higher.

"Fuck, beauty. You're stunning." I grind my hard cock into her for emphasis. "You hard, Lucas?" My brother's eyes meet mine, and he nods with a smirk, pushing himself into Tia.

"Can you feel my brother's hard cock pumping into your ass, Tia?"

She sucks in a breath and swallows.

"I bet your panties are wet, baby girl." Lucas speaks just loud enough for me to hear, then he grinds his hips into her ass.

We move with the music with the vibrations below our feet, and with the darkened atmosphere, it feels like we're in our own little bubble, like there aren't crowds of people dancing around us. Tia is sandwiched between the two of us.

"Is she wet, Cole?" Lucas stares at me daringly.

Removing my hand from her thigh, I slowly trail it up the inside of her dress and into the crotch of her panties. Pushing them aside, I'm rewarded with her wet pussy folds.

"Fuck, she's drenched." I pant the words out while my cock strains against my jeans.

"Mmm. Finger-fuck her pussy, Cole. Push them into her tight hole."

I drag my fingers down her pussy and slide two inside her. Instantly, she squeezes around me.

"Oh god." Tia launches her head back, resting it on Lucas's shoulder as I finger-fuck her pussy. My movements become more aggressive as she clenches around me and my cock leaks in my jeans.

"Fuck, brother, my cock's leaking," I admit. My eyes snap toward Lucas's. His eyes have darkened with lust. Does he feel this too? This sexual connection between us. How far would he go with sharing her?

His mouth moves toward Tia's ear, and I can just make out the words he whispers to her, "Play with his cock, Tia."

Holy fuck, I swear I squirt a bit of cum out.

Her hand grazes me over my jeans, and I close my eyes as she starts stroking me. My balls begin to draw up. Fuck no.

I snap my eyes open with a jolt. "We need to leave. Right fucking now!"

TWENTY-TWO

L ucas

His lips slam against hers as he strips her. I sit in the armchair watching, fighting with myself to join them. To show them what I want and how I want it.

But I'm frozen. So fucking frozen.

"Fuck, Tia," Cole moans as she takes hold of his thick cock. They're facing me, almost like putting a show on for me, enticing me.

My eyes travel down her body. She's perfect. Her hips are wider than the women in the porn I use to get off on, her tits are fuller in a natural way, and her nipples are darker and bigger, making me wonder if childbirth gifted her with this perfection or if she's always been this way.

"Fuck, Lucas. What should I do first?" Cole turns to face me, his eyebrows pinched together as though genuinely confused and unsure.

I swallow, slowly taking in their stunning bodies. They look perfect together. They *are* perfect together.

"Throw her on the bed and fuck her from behind. I want to see her face when you make her come."

Tia's chest rises and falls as she watches me. Her eyes are heavy and hooded, and her chest flushes as she surveys my body.

I sit back in the chair lazily, acting completely unaffected.

My white shirt is open, and my legs are wide to give my cock space. It rubs uncomfortably against my dress pants, but I refuse to acknowledge it or the pre-cum dripping from the tip.

Cole throws Tia roughly on the bed. His muscles flex with the action, and I can't help but revel in his body.

The urge to control him too and make them pay with sex for the aggression I feel is bordering on an obsession.

I lie awake at night listening to them fucking, then imagine myself orchestrating it all, forcing them to relent and concede to each of my cruel and sadistic desires.

He positions himself behind her as she clambers onto her hands and knees.

"Shove your thick cock inside her hard. Make her beg for mercy," I snipe the words out.

He rams inside her so hard my cock jumps in excitement. My blood pumps quickly around my body as Cole begins to thrust inside her.

"Fuck, she's tight, brother." His lips part on a groan.

Cole's hips hit her ass over and over, and the force hits me in the balls each and every time. My hips buck in motion with his. What I'd give to be him right now, feeling what he feels. I'd wrap her hair around my fist.

"Pull her fucking hair!"

Cole does as I ask. He takes hold of Tia's hair roughly, tugging her head back, forcing her to glare straight at me. Fuck, she looks sensational. Her nipples are peaked, and I lick my lips, wishing I could participate.

"Do you want me to come inside her or on top of her?"

My jaw tenses at the thought of him being able to do that, to experience firsthand what it must feel like to have your cock milked dry by her tight pussy.

I watch him bounce off her ass, his face contorted in ecstasy, and I lose myself. Jumping up from the chair, I stride toward the bed. Tia stares at me in shock as I flick open my knife and hold it under her chin. Cole slows his movement down, watching the exchange between us in both concern and desire.

"Keep fucking her," I snap in annoyance.

Each thrust of his is now calculated so the blade doesn't nick her skin. Tia stares at me.

"Do it. Make me bleed for you, Lucas."

My cock jumps, encouraging me to press the blade to her chin, and I watch in rapture as her skin tightens around it. Tia presses her chin down onto the metal, and a trickle of blood leaves the wound.

My eyes dilate and my nostrils flare at the sight, my blood pumps rapidly through my body, and my heart rate increases.

I'm so incredibly turned on, before I can stop myself, I snap at Cole, "Pull out!"

He pulls out of her without question.

"Lay with your head on the pillow, Tia." I nod back up toward the top of the bed, and she moves quickly.

I use the chance to undress, kicking my pants and boxers aside. Taking the knife in my hand, I climb onto the bed and position myself between her open legs, my eyes scanning over her swollen pussy lips begging for a cock to stuff her.

I take my cock in my hand, desperate to ease some of the tension building to the point of pain.

"Put your cock in her, Lucas. She wants you so fucking bad, brother."

I suck in air, desperate for it to fill my lungs, to bring me some space to breathe.

Glancing down at Tia once again, my body fills with trepidation. I shake involuntarily, regret edging to the forefront of my mind.

"Lucas." My eyes latch on to hers instantly. "Kiss me. Please."

As if magnetized, I hover my body over Tia's. Resting on my forearms, my lips find hers, and my hand tightens around my knife, clinging desperately to the only comfort I truly feel, the only sense of security I need—especially around her.

She's my salvation, but she's also the only person who could destroy me. Destroy him too. Destroy all of us. So, I grip my knife tighter for the protection I so dangerously need.

A gentle kiss causes a thousand goose bumps to break out over my body. She moans into my mouth as my tongue caresses hers.

I can feel her chest heaving, and when she drags her fingers into my hair, I press my body down on hers, molding us together. My gaze flicks over to the knife, and

Tia nods, as though she understands. I bring it to her chin and press it into the small wound from earlier, relishing in the blood flowing onto the metal.

"Mmm," she moans, making my cock jerk against her and pre-cum leak onto her stomach.

I turn to Cole. He's sitting up on the bed, watching us intently. His rock-hard cock stands tall, still wet from being inside her. "Stroke yourself."

His gaze meets mine, and he nods.

Turning back to Tia with the knowledge of Cole fucking his hand while watching us makes me want to take the next step more than anything.

I lower my mouth to her chin, stroking my tongue over the wound. A wave of urgent arousal hits me with the taste of her blood on my tongue.

"Put me inside you," I whisper.

Tia's eyebrows rise, and her hand fumbles between us as I lift up slightly to give her access.

Her hand wraps around my cock, and I close my eyes at the sensation as she positions me at her wet hole.

"Can you push inside?"

I nod against her and slowly push inside her warm pussy. My cock pulsates, and I will myself not to come, not yet.

She stretches around me, and the feeling is incredible. Never have I felt something so amazing as this. Tia clenches me as I sink farther inside her; my balls draw up, and I will them to descend.

"She feel good, brother?" Cole pants from beside me. I want to tell him to shut the fuck up, otherwise I'll come already, but feeling him brush against the sheets Tia lies on as he fists his cock excites me all the more.

My hand grips on to the knife, and Tia raises her chin for me, with steely determination in her eyes.

I place the blade beneath her, letting her choose to push down on it. A gush of wetness leaks onto my cock, and my body jolts with awareness of how much she's enjoying my knife. I pull my cock almost all the way out of her before pushing back inside. Her pussy clenches when I do it again.

My tongue replaces the knife and laps at her blood. She moans and drags her fingers through my hair. Her thighs wrap around my waist, and I find myself embracing it. My free hand finds her hip to hold her there as I fuck her.

"Fuck, brother. So damn hot."

The piercing on Cole's cock is coated in pre-cum, and I have a sudden urge to lick it clean for him, but his thumb covers it, snapping me out of the thought as he roughly fucks his hand.

I push back inside her.

"More, Lucas. Don't stop."

"Fuck," I pant, repeating my action.

My balls tingle, and her pussy seems to realize it.

"Gush on his thick cock, Tia," Cole encourages. "Show him how much you love his cock fucking you. You dirty little slut, fucking two brothers."

She tightens around me, and she throws her head back and arches on the bed, pushing her tits up toward my mouth.

"Holy shit. I'm coming!" Cole practically shouts.

I sink my teeth into the flesh of her tit as my cock begins to pulsate inside her.

"Fuck." *Slam.* "Dirty." *Slam.* "Fucking." *Slam.* "Slut." *Slam.* "Baby." *Slam.* "Girl."

My cock unloads inside her, and I crash on top of her, my head in the crook of her neck. I whisper the words for only her to hear, the ones I've been desperate to keep hidden.

"I love you."

She stills below me, but my drained body doesn't care.

I've made her mine now.

She caresses my head, running her fingers through my hair, and the feeling is hypnotic.

If only she could say those words back. Then, everything would be perfect.

She wouldn't just be his, she'd be mine too.

She'd be ours.

TIA

I wake to soft kisses being peppered over my neck and the head of a thick cock being pressed inside me.

"Mmm. Let me fuck you while you sleep, Tia." Cole groans, his hot breath against my neck.

His piercing hits me in the perfect spot, sending a wave of arousal through my entire body. I become putty in his hands, allowing him to use my body to get off as I rest lazily against Lucas's chest.

The heat from Lucas seeps into my back and the rise and fall of his breath becomes more rapid by the minute. Clearly, he's awake.

"Fuck, you feel good. Your tight little pussy is still wet with Lucas's cum, beauty."

I moan wantonly against Lucas, my hold on him tightening.

"More, Cole."

"Fuck, Lucas. You awake, brother? Our girl needs more."

As if a switch has been pressed, Lucas's eyes shoot

open, and he pulls his hand from below the pillow he's resting his head on, withdrawing it with his knife tightly in his palm. He flicks the blade open and shuffles from beneath me.

"Keep fucking her." Lucas glares toward Cole.

My clit throbs as Lucas trails the tip of the knife—not breaking the skin—along my neck, down to my breasts. He circles my nipples with the blade, and all the while, his eyes are latched firmly on mine, watching for a reaction.

Cole thrusts into me harder, and the knife nicks my skin, causing Lucas's eyes to flare at the crimson path of blood dripping onto my nipple.

"Lick it off," Cole chokes the words out as he watches from his higher angle.

Lucas moves his head closer; he switches the knife to his free hand while taking my tit in the other. He squeezes it, groping at the fullness. His eyes are wide in both awe and lust, and his face is etched in almost a pained expression.

His mouth dips to my nipple, and he sucks.

"Fuck, beauty. My brother loves sucking those big tits. Mark them, Lucas."

I feel the groan of Lucas's mouth vibrate around my peaked nipple as he suckles hard to the point of pain.

"More," I beg.

Cole moves his hand to between my legs, rubbing frantically over my clit. My eyes close on their own accord as I explode around him.

"Fuck, goddamn strangling my cock, beauty." His hand on my hip tightens.

Lucas bites my breast, and the sensation is euphoric.

"Fuck." Cole grunts as his cum spurts into my pussy, gripping his cock tightly while he pulsates inside me.

All the while, Lucas is sucking the flesh of my breast into his mouth, marking me with a sharp sting and flicking his tongue over my nipple.

I stare down at him, his eyes meeting mine beneath his long lashes. He's so hot, it should be criminal.

I drag my fingers through his hair, knowing how much he loves it.

"Fuck, brother. You should let her suck your cock. She's so good at it," Cole challenges Lucas, who has now frozen in the spot.

His hand trembles over my breast, and I want to knee Cole in the balls for unnerving him.

"You don't have to do anything you don't want to do, Lucas." I hold his gaze.

"I want to." His voice is gentle, a complete contrast to how he dominates Cole and me together. His vulnerability truly shines through when it's a physical experience of his own.

He shuffles onto his knees, putting his cock eye level with my head. I take note of his hand gripping the knife to the point of whitened knuckles.

I glance over my shoulder at Cole, who is still buried inside my pussy, his cock twitching at the sight before him.

"I might be rough." Lucas stares at me, his gaze roaming over my face, looking for a sign of discomfort.

"Good, I like it rough." I stare back at him with a challenge in my eyes.

"Teach the dirty slut a lesson, brother."

I don't miss the twitch of Lucas's cock each time Cole refers to him as brother. I'm sure he's aware of it too, and as much as it sounds fucked up, I can't help but love the sound of it.

Lucas pushes the swollen head of his cock into my mouth, barely giving me a chance to open for him. He hisses between his teeth when my tongue moves around him.

"Fuck, that's hot." Cole plays with my nipples, while rocking his growing erection in and out of me.

"Fuck, brother, go faster. I want you to cum down her throat while I cum in her pussy."

"Shit." Lucas thrusts harder, making me choke. "Fuck. That's good."

He grips my head and pushes in until I'm taking all his cock. Tears fill my eyes, and I breathe through my nose as he holds his hand firmly against my head, leaving me no room to pull back.

"Dirty fucking slut. You're going to let us brothers cum inside you, baby girl." He pulls out, giving me a chance to quickly catch my breath before surging forward. His hand fumbles with his knife, and, as though warning me, he holds the blade below my chin.

For some sick reason, the danger behind his action makes me wetter.

"You feel so incredible, baby girl."

I moan around his cock, closing my eyes as the taste of his cum coats my tongue. His rhythm becomes erratic, and he really starts to fuck my mouth hard.

"Oh fuck. Swallow it down, swallow it all down." He

pants as pleasure takes over his face, and ropes upon ropes of thick warm cum coat my tongue and throat.

"Fuck." Cole drops his head to my neck and bites me there as his own release shoots inside me once again.

Lucas's movements become slower until he eventually withdraws his cock, leaving me gasping for air. His trembling fingers trail down my cheek lovingly. "Thank you."

My tear-filled eyes glimmer in pride at the gift we've given one another.

Me, the trust to allow him the ability to do this and from him, I received the greatest gift of all: another part of him, another step closer to becoming us.

Breaking the moment, Cole leans over me and tugs my head back, slamming his lips against mine and pushing his tongue into my mouth without warning.

The bed dips, and my eyes shoot in the direction of Lucas storming from the room and slamming the door behind him.

I elbow Cole to get him off me, and I spring up from the bed. "Really, Cole? You really just kissed me with his cum in my mouth?"

Cole rolls his eyes. "I was in the moment, and it was hot." He shrugs.

Anger builds inside me at his lack of compassion, his haste to create something we all desperately want. "You're pushing things, Cole. You'll push him away."

"Yeah, well, maybe I'm fed up with only getting a piece of him. Maybe I want more."

He glares back at me with a tic in his jaw. It's the first time Cole has voiced his want for Lucas out loud.

"He wanted me before he wanted you," he snaps at me, his words wounding me and completely undermining every feeling and thought I've been experiencing.

Is Lucas using me to get to the bigger picture? Am I just a pawn in the middle of their game to get one another? My heart skips a beat.

"Shit, beauty. I'm sorry."

He moves toward me, and I take a step back. Hurt laces his face. "Please don't," he begs in bewilderment. "I can't be without you."

"I need a minute, Cole." I nibble on my lip.

"Can I kiss you?" His vulnerable eyes meet mine pleadingly. "Please?"

My heart breaks just looking at his expression. He knew instantly he'd overstepped and apologized straight away. But what hurt the most was not the feeling of being used, it was the feeling of being unwanted because separately I feel wanted. But together? We need to make that work too.

I nod toward him, and his lips clash into mine punishingly before pulling away and resting our foreheads together. "I love you, beauty. I need you to know it will always be you."

My shoulders relax at his words.

"Always." He kisses my forehead before turning and heading toward the shower.

I can't help but whisper the words I can never let him hear.

"It'll never just be you."

Because Lucas has my heart too.

TWENTY-THREE

———◆———

C ole
It's been a couple of days since I essentially licked Lucas's cum out of Tia's mouth, and the prick is still running from it.

Why the fuck he has to make such a big deal over it is beyond me. So what? It's not like I licked it from his cock, although, in that moment, if I'm honest with myself, if that's what I craved, I'd probably be down with that too.

I walk toward his office door and stroll in without knocking.

"You should knock," he spits without glancing up from his paperwork.

"Why? Don't you want me to see you tugging your cock?"

This gets his attention. I drop myself down on the swivel chair lazily with my legs apart.

"What do you want, Cole?"

"You," I reply bluntly.

He rears back in shock, his breath hitches, and his eyes search my face.

"With Tia," I tack on to help ease his obvious panic and discomfort.

I almost choke sarcastically as his shoulders relax. Would it really be so bad to want me too? "Why'd you freak out?"

Lucas's eyes narrow, and his lips tighten. He throws his pen on the desk and crosses his arms. "You really need me to answer that?"

I nod firmly. "Yeah. I do, brother." I raise an eyebrow at him.

His shoulders tighten once again, and I wince at the thought of me putting him under this discomfort, but it's a conversation we need to have. Lucas has boundaries, when I clearly have none.

He darts his eyes away from mine. "It's the first time I did that."

I watch him closely as his cheeks flush at his admittance.

"I wanted to give it to her how I wanted. I didn't want you to swoop in and take it away," he spits the words out.

I stare at him, unsure what he means.

His voice rises. "I wanted it on my terms, Cole. Mine." He stabs his finger at his chest, his face reddening in anger and the vein in his temple pulsating.

Tia's right, I pushed him too far. Too fast.

I scrub a hand over my head. "I'm sorry."

This seems to ease him.

"I need the control, Cole. If I don't have that, I don't have anything."

I want to tell him that's not true, he has us.

But that's not what he means. Not what he wants to hear. So, I bite the inside of my cheek and stay silent.

LUCAS

I scrutinize Cole's face. His muscles are bunched tight across his shirt, and his jaw clenches. I know I've hurt him. That I insulted him when I said I wanted my cum to be for Tia.

But it's true, it was meant for her.

My first time was meant for her, not him.

I stare at him, his eyes soften, and the anger behind them slowly dissipates when my words appear to register.

I snap my eyes away, unwilling to see the sympathy behind them.

Clearing my throat, I decide to change the subject. "The guy I've hired to investigate the Lancasters has said the husband"—I search the email on the screen—"Timothy Lancaster is a crooked senator. Unable to have children of his own. They originally were going to take Tia and Harper, but instead decided on only accepting Harper. We've come to the same conclusion, they figured she'd give Harper up without a fight. They offered her numerous payments."

Cole's spine straightens and his fists pump in anger.

"Obviously, she refused each and every time. The investigator has said they've made it pretty hard for her every step of the way."

"Bastards."

I glance up at Cole. "Yeah. I'm proud of her."

"They seem—" Cole pauses for a moment, as if deep in thought. "Quite old."

My eyebrows furrow in confusion as I glance back at the information sent and shake my head. "He's forty-two, and she's thirty-eight."

Cole scoffs. "She is not thirty-eight, brother." His eyes bug out. "Seriously, Lucas. Look into it more, but I'm telling you, she is not thirty-eight."

My mind begins to wander. Maybe they put down a younger age on the form so they stand a better chance of gaining custody of Harper?

"Okay, I'll have him investigate that too."

"When's Rage back? It's like you sent the poor dude on a road trip to bumfuck nowhere. He's been blowing up my phone, pissed you're arranging more things for him."

My body tightens at Cole's words. I brush an uneasy hand through my hair, my throat suddenly feeling dry and my chest constricting.

"Wednesday, next week."

Cole, oblivious to my internal meltdown, checks his phone. "Good. I'm fed up with having to run the gym and the club. I want some time with Tia." He gazes up from his phone and stares at me. A heavy thickness of longing hangs in the air, an undercurrent of sexual tension. I can read his mind, hear what he's saying without him actually saying it. Without him uttering a single word. "And you, I want you too."

I nod in understanding.

Cole stands and brushes his palms over his legs, and my eyes track the movement. His thick thighs fill his jeans tightly.

When he clears his throat, I snap my gaze up toward his cocky grin. "I'll see you later, brother." He winks before leaving the office, leaving me with a rock-hard cock and a mind full of uncertainty.

How far am I willing to go?

How far will he let me?

TWENTY-FOUR

Tia

I throw my pencil down on the table. There's something missing from the image, but I can't figure out what, and it's driving me insane. I stare at the princess on the paper and the ring the prince holds. But every fairytale has the ring and the prince. I need mine to be different.

"Urgh!" I scream loudly and push away from the table.

I need a change of scenery; I need to get out of here and find something to do.

Finding myself outside Lucas's office door, I'm about to knock when it opens. My breath hitches with his closeness, his cologne filling my nostrils. I tilt my head up toward him. His gray eyes bore into mine like he wants to eat me alive, and I lick my lips at the thought.

"Baby girl." His chest rises rapidly, giving away his own excitement at our close proximity. He gently tucks a wave of my hair behind my ear.

His words breeze over me. "Did you want something?"

I want to scream, *you*. I want to wrap my arms around his neck and climb him like a goddamn tree. But I don't want to freak him out. So instead, I opt for the easier option. "I'm bored."

He quirks a brow in amusement. "Bored?"

"Yes. Bored, Lucas. I need to get out of here." I wave my hand down the corridor toward the apartment door.

His eyebrows knit together as though deep in thought.

"Where's Cole?"

"The gym. Training." His clipped tone tells me he's still sour.

"Can we go?"

"You want to go to the gym?"

"I want to go and watch Cole train, yes."

His eyes travel up and down my body, and his lip tugs up at the side. "Let's go." He pulls his car keys from his pocket and takes my hand, leading me toward the apartment door.

"Should I change?"

Lucas stops walking and turns his head, scanning my body once again.

"No."

I quickly flick my eyes down my outfit. Yoga pants and a cropped top. I shrug a shoulder, *meh*. Kind of gym wear.

COLE

"No. You dumbass motherfucker, you're not goddamn listening. When I said dropkick, I meant dropkick. Here, let me show you."

I get into position on the mat before demonstrating the perfect dropkick. "Now, try a-fucking-gain."

My eyes latch on to the doors opening, and every head in the room turns in the same direction. Lucas walks in like he owns the place, which I guess he does, but it's what's behind him that piques my interest.

Tia.

Every goddamn muscle in my body bunches tight when I see what she's wearing: yoga pants and a cropped top that exposes her toned stomach and perfect figure.

Her nipples poke through her top, and my jaw locks in rage. What the fuck is she thinking? And what the fuck is Lucas thinking bringing her here like that?

I scowl in his direction to see he's watching and waiting for a reaction from me. The fucker did this on purpose, brought her here half-dressed so every fucker can have their greedy eyes on my girl.

"Cole?"

I breathe through my nostrils, then I stride toward the ropes and jump over them. I roughly take a hold of her hand, making her eyes widen, but I choose to ignore her shocked expression.

I head to the back gym room and yell, "Every fucker out!" My chest heaves in rage, and the sweat clinging to my skin only adds to my heightened temper.

The guys grumble and groan before doing as I ask and leaving the room. As the door clicks shut, I stare at Lucas. A smug smile spreads over his face as I glare at him.

"This what you wanted?"

I swipe the dripping sweat from my forehead with my palm. "You want me pissed?"

He takes a step forward and casts Tia a quick glance. "You can see her nipples through her top."

"I'm aware," I snap back at him; my teeth grind at the thought of others seeing my girl like this.

"You said I looked okay," she throws in his direction, shock lacing her words.

Lucas smirks.

Yeah, the fucker knows exactly what he's doing. He orchestrated this to get a rise out of me, no doubt to punish me too.

Well, I'm about to turn shit around on him.

"I think she needs punishing, Lucas. Leaving the apartment dressed like this." I tweak her nipple through her top, making her wince with a jolt. "Letting everyone look at what's ours." I cast my gaze above Tia toward Lucas. "Letting everyone think she's a whore. When she's our whore. Ours." I grab her by her ponytail and crash my lips to hers.

Her hands roam over my sweaty chest, over my abs, and up and down my neck, as though she's desperate to touch me. I grind my cock into her harder, eliciting a moan from her greedy lips. "Fuck. I bet you're so wet, beauty."

"I bet her cunt's dripping for our cum, Cole." Lucas steps forward, unbuckling his belt lazily, whereas I'm desperate to rip her top from her tits and shove my cock into her so hard she feels me for a lifetime.

"Strip her and put her on the bench press." He snaps the belt, and the sound makes my cock jump in anticipation.

Fuck me, his dominance is such a turn-on.

Tia's chest begins to rise, and heat travels up to her cheeks. She's so damn cute.

I grab her roughly and spin her around so her back is to us. I grip her yoga pants and tear them down her legs. She kicks her shoes off, and I pull the pants free from her feet.

Lucas moves to position himself in front of her, and I watch in complete awe as he flicks open his blade and trails it down her chest, causing goose bumps to spread over her exposed body.

I watch in elation as Lucas cuts her top down the middle and then the straps, causing her heavy tits to

229

bounce. I take a hold of her hips and grind my cock into her ass, reveling in the friction of my piercing against the material of my shorts.

"Fuck," I grunt.

Lucas's eyes meet mine, his hooded with desire. His top two shirt buttons are open, leaving his chest slightly exposed, and I long to reach out and touch him.

I grind into her again. "Oh god, Cole."

"Dirty little fucking whore." Lucas's eyes darken on his words, and his face contorts. "Our toy to use and abuse. Now, lie with your stomach on the bench, baby girl." He trails a finger down her cheek tenderly, as though he hadn't just called her a whore.

Lucas moves aside, his tented pants on full display.

Tia lays over the bench, her head almost hanging over the side. Lucas steps up behind her and kicks her feet apart, exposing her asshole, and I almost come in my shorts.

"Get your cock out, Cole." Lucas glares at me.

Without thinking, I fumble with the waistband, tugging my cock over the top and leaving my balls tucked beneath the waistband. I stroke my hand lazily up and down to take the edge off, the tip of my cock glistening with pre-cum.

"I need a safe word from you, baby girl," he coos as he trails that knife of his down her spine so gently, it doesn't break the skin; his eyes are transfixed on the tip of the blade, and his voice has a dark, gritty edge to it.

I wonder how far Lucas would go if his self-restraints let him?

"Red."

"Now, I'm going to whip your ass raw and then Cole is going to fuck you."

Before Tia can respond, he lifts the belt and smacks it down hard on her ass, making her jolt at the force. The sound of the belt hitting her skin makes my cock spurt.

"Fuck, that's good." I swipe the cum over my piercing and use my thumb to press on it, forcing me to thrust into my tightened fist. "Mmm, fuck."

A swish in the air jolts me to watch as Lucas slaps the belt against her firm ass another two times.

"Oh god, Lucas."

"You want me to stop?" He smacks her with it again.

Tia shakes her head.

"Use your fucking words. You want me to stop whipping your ass like the dirty little whore you are?"

"No. I can take it."

"Yes, you can take it. You can take me whipping your ass raw and Cole shoving his big cock inside your pussy while I pin you down. Can't you, baby girl?"

"Yes."

Smack!

"Are you wet?" He puts two fingers together then brutally shoves them inside her pussy. I fuck my hand harder when he withdraws them with Tia's slick juices coating his fingers. "Dirty little whore likes being punished."

Lucas grazes his fingers over her ass before stopping at her puckered hole. "Anyone fuck this?" he questions, snapping his head up toward hers.

"No." Her words come out breathy and needy, and I want nothing more than to fuck her hard.

Lucas's mouth drops open, and he moves his hand to pump his cock through his pants. He bites his bottom lip as though struggling to restrain himself.

Then, he swallows thickly and tilts his head back toward the ceiling, his eyes closed.

After getting himself together, Lucas stares back at Tia's ass, grazing a palm over it tenderly. "Good. I decide who fucks your ass and when. Do you understand?"

"Y . . . yes."

Lucas lifts the belt and gives her ass another two lashes. Her spine arches, and her toes curl.

"Good. Baby girl. So good," he coos gently as his palms breeze over her reddened ass cheeks.

He turns his gaze to me, his eyes dark with desire and a deadly edge tinged in them. "Cole, fuck her hard. I want her pussy raw and dripping."

I nod at his words, so turned on I'm unable to talk. He moves to stand in front of Tia while I move to stand in between Tia's legs.

"Fuck her." He stares at me from under his lashes as his deep, dominant voice commands my body until I don't even recognize it belongs to me anymore. I slam inside her so hard, Lucas has to pin her shoulders down so she doesn't shift off the bench.

"Oh shit, Cole," Tia pants.

I pull out and repeat the action. Her warm, wet pussy tries to pull me back in. "Fuck, you feel good, beauty."

Slam.

"So fucking good." I groan when my piercing hits the wall of her cervix, and the thought makes my balls draw up, leaving me no choice but to pull almost all the way out and my hand to rise, slapping it down hard on her ass as punishment.

"You're our whore to fuck, beauty. Nobody else's." *Slam.* "Ours." *Slam.*

I grab hold of her ponytail, tugging her head back sharply. I don't miss the wince that falls from her lips.

"Now, be a good baby girl," I mock, "and tell Daddy you want your mouth stuffed with his fat cock."

Lucas's face drains of all anger. Instead, it morphs into sheer amazement, as though a realization has taken place before he effortlessly pulls the mask of dominance back on. The mask hiding the vulnerability, insecurity, and lack of hands-on experience.

"Daddy's going to stuff that pretty little mouth now, baby girl."

Tia moans in pleasure at our words, and her pussy leaks so much she drenches my balls. "She likes you saying 'Daddy,' brother. She just soaked my balls."

Lucas grunts, quickly unzipping his pants with shaky hands, and withdraws his cock out. Strings of pre-cum drip from it, making my cock jolt in arousal.

"Fuck, brother. I won't last much longer." I slam into her again.

Lucas smirks at me in response. "Open."

Tia lifts her chin, and I tug her head back for him. He closes his eyes as he eases into her mouth. Fuck me, this is hot. I groan when Tia clenches around me.

Her muffled moans spur me on as I watch my brother fuck his baby girl's mouth with his fat cock. Each time he pulls out, her saliva is coating his cock. I ram inside her harder, forcing her to jolt against his groin. Lucas takes the opportunity to hold her head there, so I let go of her ponytail and watch in complete awe as I fuck her, with my hands on her reddened ass. I stare down at the markings on her ass and pull her cheeks apart to look at her tight little virgin hole. Jesus, I need that too.

Sweat coats my skin as I try to delay my orgasm, slowing down, then having no choice but to speed up.

Tia tightens around me.

Slam.

"Lucas, fuck, I'm going to . . ."

Slam.

"Pull out before you fully empty, I want it on her ass too."

I groan, and my head drops back at the sensation of her tight pussy milking me.

My cock swells, and cum spurts from the engorged tip.

"Fuuuuuuck."

Before my orgasm ends, I pull out and watch myself fist my cock over her bouncing ass cheeks. Fuck, that's hot.

Lucas's eyes are trained on the action too, making me come even harder.

"Come here and let her lick your cock clean while I feed her pussy my cum."

Jesus. His words send a bolt of excitement to my balls.

We swap ends, and I stare in amazement as Lucas rubs my cum into her ass. Then, he stares straight into my eyes, causing my heart to skip a beat. "I'm going to push your cum inside her, brother."

I swallow hard. The thought of him using my cum is enough to make my dick harden. Tia opens her mouth and begins lapping her tongue over my cock.

"The slit, beauty. Do the slit." I hiss between my teeth when she gently tugs on my piercing. I shove my cock into her mouth. She gags, but I hold her head still and force her to take me. Her tongue swirls in every direction around my length.

Lucas has his knife clutched in his palm. His eyes are fixed on the tip of the blade, and I can't help but wonder what he's thinking. The crazed look in his eyes tell me he's battling with himself over something.

Tia moans, the vibration incredible around me.

"Ah, fuck."

Lucas picks up his pace, but he still stares at the knife, debating with himself.

"Do it." He snaps his eyes up to mine. "Whatever you're thinking. Do it," I encourage, determined to help him break down his walls.

His shoulders ease slightly, as though accepting what he's about to do. With his cock still shoved inside Tia, he presses down on the skin above her ass, cutting into her. She whimpers around my cock, and I hold her head tighter, giving her no room for movement as I watch in rapture when he engraves his and my name into her flesh.

I stroke over Tia's hair, occasionally grinding my cock

into her but no longer forceful, because at the sight of mine and his name marking her lower back, my cum floods her mouth, and when Lucas smears her blood over her ass, he comes too with a loud groan.

"Fuck. Daddy loves you, baby girl."

TWENTY-FIVE

Cole

I had to dig some clothes out of my locker for Tia to wear so none of those gym fuckers could witness my beauty in her bare flesh.

She was so exhausted from our time with her, she laid curled up in Lucas's arms all the way home.

I watched in the rearview mirror while I drove us back to the apartment how he cradled her, as though she's a precious gift. He gently stroked her hair and dropped gentle pecks of his lips onto her head, and all the while, she laid there with her eyes closed, as though completely content in his arms.

When I opened the car door and reached for Tia, he shouldered past me like a pissed-off child and then barked orders at me to run her a bath with oils while he rocked her in his arms, as though she was damaged in some way. As though it wasn't us who fucked her roughly into unconsciousness.

I stripped down when Lucas demanded I get in the

bath with Tia, and only then did he hand her to me after he lifted her arms like a child and tugged the shirt from her body.

Tia's eyes lazily searched around the room before landing on me with a look of content. She took my hand in hers and stepped into the tub, allowing me to wash her body under Lucas's watchful scrutiny.

I lather the sponge and follow Lucas's instructions without question.

He helped her out and he wrapped her up in a thick white towel while I mused whether to follow or see to my hard cock.

When he snapped my name, I jumped out of the tub like a good little lapdog. Grabbing a towel, I wrap it around my waist and join them in the bedroom. My bedroom.

Tia is lying on her stomach, her naked form filling my cock and making my balls heavy. Lucas palms her red, welted ass cheeks tenderly, rubbing something that looks like ointment into her skin.

He then traces over the engraved names resting above her ass, with his fingertip coated in the same substance.

Tia flinches, causing Lucas to coo in her direction, his tone of voice reserved purely for her. "Shh, baby girl. Let Daddy take care of you."

His eyes are transfixed lovingly on her, as though she's his whole world, while I stand leaning against the doorframe, hanging back and looking in on their time together like an outsider in my own room.

An intruder in their relationship. I swallow thickly at

the thought. A heavy weight no longer in my balls but now sitting in my stomach threatens to make my heart explode into a million pieces. It constricts when his fingers glide over her spine and he peppers kisses into her hair.

"Such a good girl."

My fists ball with anger. I gave him this. I gave him her, and now, I'm standing on the sidelines looking in.

When he leans over and drops loving words in her ear, I can't stand it anymore. I storm past them and head toward the kitchen.

My temple pulsates, and my shoulders bunch tight as I pull the fridge open and take out a beer. Flipping the cap, I down it in one and then grab another. Just as I lift the bottle to my lips, Lucas appears.

I can sense his eyes on me, but I choose to ignore him. Instead, I close my eyes and tip the beer back. The cold liquid doesn't so much as quench my need right now.

"Problem?" His deep voice sends a shiver through my veins, but I ignore him and continue drinking.

"I asked you a fucking question, Cole."

My eyes pop open in annoyance, and I slam the bottle onto the counter and turn to face him. I can feel my face redden in anger, and I struggle to control the rise in my voice. "You don't get to speak to me like that outside of the bedroom, Lucas. I might allow you to dominate in there, but out here, we're equals."

Lucas steps back as though my words have thrown him. I watch as he drags a hand through his hair, and his chest rises rapidly, but I ignore the feeling of him being hurt at my outburst and continue on with my own.

"She's mine, Lucas, and I allow you to share her, so don't push me fucking out!"

My words vibrate off the walls.

"I . . . I didn't. I wasn't . . . That's not what I was doing."

I step closer to him, and he steps back.

"Yes you fucking were. She's mine to care for too." I poke my finger into my chest. "All 'Daddy looks after you' bullshit. You'd never have dared utter those fucking words if I hadn't said them."

Lucas's face pales, and I feel a brief flicker of guilt pang at my heart.

"I could take her away if I wanted to." I smirk at him like an ass.

Out of the corner of my eye, I catch movement, and when I turn my head, I see the heartbroken expression of Tia. Her eyes are filled with unshed tears, and the bedsheet is tugged so tightly around her, I don't miss the whites of her knuckles gripping it as though it's a barrier between us. My heart sinks at her expression.

Shit. I fucked up.

I move my feet in her direction, but she puts her hand up to stop me moving further forward.

"The only person I belong to, Cole, is me." A tear falls from her eye, but she makes no effort to remove it from her cheek. "I get to decide. Not you. Not him."

The double-ended meaning of the word *him* floods my blood with rage. She isn't referring to Lucas—or maybe she is? But deep down, I know she's referring to the man who hurt her, and that thought alone feels like a knife through my heart.

"I want to be alone tonight." She stares down at the ground, her eyes empty, causing panic to whirl inside me. I can feel the tension and turmoil vibrating off Lucas; he's unraveling by the second, the thought of losing her too much to bear. What the fuck have I done? All because I had a moment of jealousy.

She turns and heads toward the spare room, the one we plan on turning into a bedroom for Harper.

"Lucas, I . . ."

His eyes snap to mine, hate glaring from them, and the tremble in his voice proves he's struggling. "Fix it!"

He strides away toward his office, slamming the door behind him and leaving me standing there, wondering where the hell tonight went wrong.

TIA

I lie in bed with my finger trailing over the soft cotton sheets in rhythmic circles, much like I used to do to Jace as a teenager.

I can't ignore how my mind immediately goes to the last person who hurt me—truly hurt me—and yet I shouldn't link them together with the hurt Cole caused last night.

He spoke about me as though I was an object, a toy, a tool in his plan, not the woman he loves and wants to build a life with.

This whole scenario was his idea, and now, he's pissed that Lucas is finally finding his place in our relationship. He's soon gone from being supportive to being set on destroying us.

I've barely slept a wink all night; hurt laced my body, the same body I let them use and mark. Sure, I loved every second of it, but for the night to turn out the way it did makes me resent each and every touch from both their bodies.

The door creaks open, but I pay it no attention, not even when I feel the mattress beside me dip and the scent of Cole reaches my nose.

My spine straightens when he touches me. He braces his arm around my waist and pulls me tightly into him, my back to his chest.

His breath whispers against my ear, "I'm sorry, beauty."

I shake my head and try to pull away, annoyed that he thinks he can just crawl back into bed with me and everything will be okay.

"Stop." He holds me in a firm grip and I feel him swallow against my neck. "I was jealous." His heart rate picks up. "I was being a jealous dick, and I didn't think you needed me anymore, and I couldn't bear it." His voice tremors ever so slightly, giving away the truth behind his words.

I roll over to face him and search his crumbled, despairing face. Slowly, I glide my fingers over his jawline, sensing the vulnerability oozing from him, and I hate it, hate the thought of him and Lucas hurting. And just like that, I'm encompassed in him once again, and the need to reassure him tugs heavily in my chest.

"We're a package deal, Cole. I'll never pick just one. Never. For this to work, you need to believe it." I swallow before continuing, "We all do. Otherwise, it'll never work."

His eyes search my face, and his shoulders relax. "I don't want to be on the outside, Tia. I want to care for you too."

My body melts at his words. Not long ago, I had

nobody looking out for me, nobody to protect or care for me, and now, I not only have one man completely devoted to me, I have two. We just have to find the correct balance for this to work.

My hand finds his face, his touch sending familiar tingles over my body. His scent invades my nostrils, and a rush of sickness overwhelms me. I can only imagine it's at the thought of losing him, and I hate that.

"You're irreplaceable, Cole Maguire. When I had nothing, you gave me hope. When I needed support, you gave me love, and when I was aroused, you gave me a million orgasms."

His lips kick up in his signature cocky grin.

My heart races at my own words. "I promise you, you're mine as much as I'm yours. I love you, Cole."

His forehead drops to mine.

"I love you too, beauty. So fucking much it hurts."

My breath stutters at the look of devotion on his face.

His soft lips find mine, and once again, I'm transported to a place of love and care. Where his devotion is as brutal as it is loving.

CHAPTER
TWENTY-SIX

———✦———

C ole

I hadn't realized we'd fallen asleep until I felt the bed dip and a shuffle of sheets. My eyes flick open, and I stare directly into Lucas's. Relief coats his features, and he stares at me as he drops a gentle kiss to Tia's cheek resting on my chest.

My heart hammers at his proximity, and I scan his naked chest, wondering if he's completely naked and as hard as me right now. He smirks as though reading my mind, causing my Adam's apple to bob in my suddenly dry throat.

He dips his head down, and before I realize what's happening, he disappears beneath the sheets. I can feel his body move around me, and my cock throbs with thoughts he's not ready for, possibly ever.

Tia jolts, her nails dig into my chest, and her eyes dart open before she lets out a soft moan that can only be caused by the lapping noises now coming from below us both. I lay stoically still, unsure of what to do.

I stare down at Tia when her delicate lips drop open, and, feeling the need to do something, I thrust my thumb into her mouth. Her tongue swirls around it, sucking harder as her body begins to writhe on top of mine.

My solid cock weeps, and my muscles bunch with need. Tia must sense my unraveling because her soft hand wraps around my cock, and she begins to pump me as she grinds against Lucas's mouth.

"Does he feel good, beauty? Is he licking your pussy good?"

"Y . . . yes." She pants the words out as she works my cock faster, both of us unraveling.

"Fuck, brother. You must be eating her pussy so damn good. She's strangling my cock." I thrust into her hand, helping her fuck me. Her thumb swipes over my piercing, and I can't help the groan that leaves my mouth when she plays with it. Her mouth vibrates over my thumb, and I quickly swap it out for my tongue. She mingles hers with mine and sucks on the piercing.

Tia moves her hips and hand faster, groaning comes from Lucas, and before I know what's happening, Tia stills on a low moan that forces me to thrust into her palm harder. I take hold of her hand and tighten it in my fist, creating a vise so I can release over us both. My head drops against the pillow, but Tia crashes her mouth against mine once again as my cock pulses under our joined fists.

Lucas pulls himself from beneath the covers, tugging the sheet off us both in the process. I'm unsure whether he meant to, but when his eyes lock on to my cum-coated abs and they alight with desire, I'm pretty damn sure he loves the fact I got off as much as Tia did.

His tussled dark hair covers his eyes, and his mouth is coated in our girl's juices, making me want to reach out and lick it from his face. My hand twitches to pull him toward me.

"Tia." His deep, commanding voice draws our eyes to his. "Lick Cole clean, baby girl."

Without hesitation, Tia rolls onto her stomach with her ass facing Lucas, who is now essentially between my legs too. She lowers her face and swipes her tongue over my balls, up my cock, and over my abs, cleaning up my cum.

"Good girl, beauty." I stroke over her hair while my eyes stay locked on Lucas and his dripping cock; it's thick and angry looking, and with Lucas's lust-filled eyes, I can tell he's desperate to release. He moves behind Tia, and I tilt my head up to watch him enter her from behind.

I feel every jolt deep inside my balls as Tia's moans make my cock harder.

"Fuck, baby girl." He slaps her ass, and she whimpers—no doubt from being tender. I grip her hair tighter with excitement. "Daddy's little girl cleaning up my brother's mess." He raises his hand and smacks it down hard on her ass, making her flinch.

My hold on her head tightens when she positions my cock in her throat. My eyes glaze over. "Fuck, brother. She's swallowing my cock down like such a good girl."

Lucas works his hips faster, and the movement of his legs against mine makes me ram my cock into Tia harder.

My eyes lock with his, his jaw tight and his face contorted in desperation.

"Fuck, brother. Give it to me," I speak directly to him. The look of pleasure on his face makes my balls draw up, my hand still in her hair.

He rams into her one final time before his movements stutter and his mouth drops open.

"Fuck, Cole." His words are a lifeline; they're spoken to me. Directly to me. He wants me. He wants us, and they're both a blessing and a curse because I'm not sure Lucas is ever going to truly accept his feelings toward me.

Toward us.

TWENTY-SEVEN

Lucas

I move quickly in the bathroom, adjusting the package before placing it in the makeup bag. I fold the towels as always and place Cole's boxers into the dirty wash hamper.

"Hey, brother. Are you okay?"

I turn to Cole, and he scans over me before analyzing my face. I thought I'd done a pretty good job of disguising my nervousness, but clearly not.

He stands leaning against the door frame with his arms crossed over his chest, his ability to take my breath away at every turn not lost on me.

"Why wouldn't I be?" I dart my eyes away quickly, and I imagine a smug grin encompassing his face.

He breathes out deeply. I'm not sure if it's in annoyance or uncertainty. "You seem a little . . . off this morning."

"Off?"

"Yeah. You good with what happened last night?" He

drags his hand over his cropped hair, suddenly uncomfortable. I rearrange his toiletries on the bathroom counter. "With us." I turn to him, and a need to put his mind at rest hits me straight in the chest.

"I enjoyed it." I stare into his green eyes, hoping he can see the truth behind my words. His shoulders relax, and a smile plays on his lips.

"Me too. I came so fucking hard."

It's my turn to smirk now because the look of euphoria on Cole's face when he came to me saying his name was like a fucking dream. Controlling him. Controlling both of them.

My eyes shutter closed on the memory ingrained in my brain, the feeling so intense, I can feel it clawing to get out, clawing for more. More control, more of my filthy words, and the desperate need to fill her while controlling Cole's pleasure too, then allowing him to fill Tia's pussy. Flooding it with our cum. Our seed.

"Yeah. You're definitely acting weird."

I snap my gaze open to watch him turn to leave, but his absence is soon filled with Tia.

"Oh. You don't have to tidy this bathroom, Lucas. I can do it." She takes Cole's shirt from the counter and dumps it in the hamper with a playful huff.

"I always do it," I admit quietly.

Tia stops beside me. "You do?"

"I like the place clean. Cole and Rage are . . ." My words trail off while I try to think of the correct word.

"Messy?" she prompts.

"Disgusting."

Tia scoffs on a laugh but then she raises her eyebrows

when she realizes I'm being serious, leading me to admit their previous plans. "They wanted a cleaner. I don't like people in my space."

Tia smiles softly in understanding. "Well, I can help you now. I don't mind cleaning." She nibbles at her lip nervously. "Maybe you should do Rage's, though, in case he's not comfortable with me being in his space."

I almost want to choke on her words. Of course he'll be comfortable with her in his space.

Who wouldn't be?

She's perfect.

"What time are you expecting him?" She glances back at the door, as though he's going to walk through it at any moment.

"He's going to be here for dinner."

She wrings her hands with a tremble. "I hope he likes me."

My eyes narrow because what's not to like?

I crowd her against the wall. "As long as Cole and I like you, baby girl, that's the main thing."

My lips breeze over hers, and her soft fingers take hold of my jaw as I frantically unbuckle my belt with a determined need to fill her. Reassure her.

My anxiety of the situation fills me with a need to prove to her how much I want her. How much she means to me.

"Please." She whimpers into our kiss. "Please, Daddy." Holy fuck, my cock weeps at the term of endearment.

"Baby girl." I push her panties aside and surge inside her warm, slick pussy.

Our tongues wrestle furiously as I take hold of her throat and press so hard, her head drops back against the wall, and her pussy clenches around me. I release her so I can suck on her neck and leave marks. I want everyone to see she belongs to me. That I did this.

I created this relationship. Me.

I come so hard I bite into her tender flesh and revel in the copper taste on my tongue, determined to leave yet another mark on her.

Just to be certain he knows she's ours.

Staring down into her blue eyes, I can't help but tell her one more time before it all goes to shit.

My heart hammers rapidly against my chest, and my hold on her hips tighten, scared to lose her already. "I love you, baby girl." My words are heartfelt, filled with so much love and emotion, her eyes fill with tears. "Promise me you won't leave and hurt him."

Tia's eyebrows draw together in confusion.

"Promise me you'll love Cole, no matter what," I beg because the thought of breaking my brother's heart along with my own is too much to bear.

A soft smile graces her lips, and her shoulders relax.

"I love you too, Lucas." Her fingers glide down my face and over my jaw. "You and Cole. I'll never leave either one of you. I promise."

Her words hit me in the chest so hard I struggle for air.

How I've longed to hear those words. I've been desperate to hear them, to feel the warmth when they fall from her lips and seep into my bones, and today, of all days, she uses them without realizing those very words are a lie.

Because by the end of today, Tia will hate me.

There's not a doubt in my mind.

I can only hope she'll love Cole enough for the both of us.

CHAPTER
TWENTY-EIGHT

Cole

Lucas has been anxious all day. I haven't missed the tugging on his hair and the pacing whenever he's not busying himself.

I sit, watching his leg bounce, trying to figure out why the hell he's getting so worked up over Rage coming home.

When he texted earlier to say he was going straight to the club instead of the family meal Tia prepared for us all, I was pissed.

We haven't seen him in weeks now, and I'm desperate for him to finally meet my girl—our girl—and for him to accept her.

Accept us.

Lucas must be agitated. Coming out as having a relationship for the first time in his life must be hard. Coupled with the fact he's in a ménage of some sort, I can understand his anxieties. Rage sure as shit isn't going to be supportive of us, and the thought angers me.

Since his girl did the dirty on him years ago, he refuses to acknowledge any woman worth bothering with beyond a release. I clench my fists in annoyance.

I push back from my chair and jump to my feet. "I'm going to the club to fetch him."

Tia's widened eyes dart to mine.

Lucas stands. "Me too." His tongue darts out over his lips, his pale face making me glare at him in annoyance that he's letting Rage get to him this way.

"Beauty, go take a bath. We'll be back soon." I bend and drop a kiss to her head.

Lucas follows suit, but he lingers with uncertainty. I take in his shaky hand and hate that he's feeling this way.

My jaw locks as I stride toward the door. Time to sort this shit out with our brother.

RAGE

The bitch attached to my cock makes grunting noises as if she's in a damn trough scoffing pellets, not lavishing my cock with love.

My jaw locks in anger, and I grip her hair with my fist and ram into her mouth, so fucking hard my teeth feel like they're going to shatter.

Her hair feels wrong in my hand; it's coarse and thick, and the color's all wrong too. So, I do what I always do when I need a release. I close my eyes and imagine I'm fucking someone else.

She makes scoffing noises that raise the hairs on my neck, setting my body on edge.

"Shut the fuck up and suck." I grit the words out like a bastard and finally delight in the sound of her choking. At least now she can't make those god-awful desperate noises that are meant to turn me on.

My office door swings open and bounces off the wall, making my eyes dart over to the fucker who dared to interrupt me without knocking.

Correction, two fuckers.

My cock deflates under the disapproving look on Lucas's face while Cole looks damn right pissed. Which is odd, considering how much he appreciates a cock sucker.

I push the woman away and painstakingly shove my semi-hard cock into my jeans.

"Come back later," I snap at her without giving her a second glance. A sliver of guilt runs through me as the fake blonde glares in my direction before she sashays out the door.

How can I feel guilty even now when I fuck someone? It's like she owns a part of me, and I hate her for it. My hands ball into fists and the bubble of resentment I feel inside threatens to resurface.

"You were meant to be home for dinner," Cole aims in my direction while he lazily throws himself on the couch. The heat of his glare penetrates into my heart, but I choose to ignore it. Instead, I opt to glare back at him, edging for a fight. Maybe then I'll feel better.

I narrow my eyes on him. "The last thing I wanted to do was come home and have to play happy fucking families. I've been away forever."

"Slight exaggeration," Lucas mumbles loud enough for us to hear.

Cole sighs heavily and drags a hand over the top of his cropped head.

"We've something to tell you." The nervousness in his voice cannot be missed. My eyes dart toward Lucas's, and only now do I take him in. He leans stoically still against the wall farthest away from me, a lurker as usual, but something is off with him tonight, as he stares at the floor, unwilling to make eye contact with me.

What the fuck has been happening while I've been gone?

My back straightens when my thoughts immediately go to what I've asked of Lucas, my mouth suddenly dry. I open my mouth to speak the words.

"Me and Lucas. We're . . . errr . . ."

Glancing back at Cole, I realize, once again, I'm riddled with disappointment. Lucas has no news for me.

"We're . . . erm . . ."

Whatever Cole is struggling with is big because I've never seen the idiot so damn nervous and unsure of himself.

"We're both fucking Tia." Lucas steps forward, finishing Cole's sentence for him, and, holy shit, what the fuck did he just say? My mouth drops open. Surely he doesn't mean . . .?

"We're both in a relationship with Tia," he repeats, with more clarity this time.

My eyes widen in shock. Because how the hell do you go from fucking nobody—ever—to fucking the same girl as your brother?

My mind races wondering what exactly he means, what exactly he's trying to say. "Like together?"

"We don't fuck one another. We fuck her," Lucas snaps.

I throw myself back in my chair and laugh. It sounds sadistic as fuck, even to my ears. But who the hell would have thought when my brother finally popped his fucking cherry, he did it with the same girl who brought Cole to his knees?

"Must be some good pussy." I smirk in their direction and don't miss when their bodies tighten on my words.

"We love her," Cole clips back at me, his dark tone a warning, one I understand all too well. He doesn't want me to disrespect her.

I nod in acknowledgment. "Got it."

Both of them seem to relax at the same time. It would be comical if it wasn't so insane.

I haven't missed the glances Lucas shoots Cole's way; I can see the longing in his eyes, but I also see the fear. I'm not sure my brother will ever be able to own up to the fact that he might love this girl, but he loves my brother like that too.

Maybe this is his way of getting close to Cole. His way of being accepted.

Lucas clears his throat. "She's waiting." He glares at me once again, making me roll my eyes.

Jumping to my feet, I tug on my leather jacket.

"Let's go meet the woman who brought my brothers to their knees." I slap a hand on each of their shoulders as we walk toward the office door. "You never know, guys, I might just snag her right from under you."

A tremor passes over Lucas, making me throw my head back on a laugh.

Not a fucking chance in hell.

I hate all women.

All of them.

CHAPTER
TWENTY-NINE

—✦—

Rage

The anxiety bouncing off Lucas as the elevator travels up toward our penthouse apartment is unmistakable, and I can't help but feel guilty that I helped create that for him. Cole can sense it too; his eyes are filled with pity, and they keep drifting toward him followed by a childish glare in my direction, letting me know I caused this whole fucked-up situation.

I refuse to acknowledge the fact, instead resting lazily against the wall until the elevator comes to a stop. I push off and head toward the door.

"Cole. Cole, I . . ." Lucas attempts to speak to Cole, but his words are lost, and he doesn't manage to formulate a sentence. His face is ghastly pale, making me for the first time think there's more to his behavior than meets the eye.

Cole grips Lucas by the neck, pulling him in so his forehead rests against his. It doesn't look like a lover's embrace, so I watch on.

"It's okay, brother. We got this." Cole grins, but Lucas shakes his head, refusing to listen.

I choose to ignore their little tiff and open the apartment door. The first thing to fill my nostrils is something of nostalgia, but I can't quite place what it is—something Italian smelling—making regret hang heavily in my stomach when I realize the effort my brothers have gone to for my homecoming. They know Italian food is my favorite.

Cole pushes past me. "Rage, this is Tia. Our Tia."

I turn toward him, and my eyes instantly clash with those so familiar to me, my heart feels like it's being ripped from my chest. I can't breathe, and my mind floats somewhere so high I can't reach it. My legs weaken as my chest tightens, air sucked so forcefully from my lungs, I lose all power and drop to my knees on a deafening wail.

It takes me so long to realize it's not my wail. Not my voice. It's hers.

The same one I drove away from five years ago. The same voice that ripped out my heart and shredded it to pieces, leaving it so mangled, not another living soul could get close enough again.

"Lucas? Lucas, what the hell's happening?" Cole is crying above her, but I can't move. My head is dropped to the ground, and my fists are balled tight as I kneel on the floor, shutting out everything around me.

This can't be real. This can't be her.

With them?

My head suddenly snaps up at the realization.

She's with them.

Rage fills my body, anger like nothing before. I see red, red so fucking deep there's never going to be enough blood to drain from their bodies.

I fly toward Cole. He's cradling her in his arms. He's cradling what's mine.

Mine!

Lucas tackles me to the ground; he's so quick, I forgot he was even here.

"Take her to the spare room. Now!" he screams toward Cole, who rushes away with my girl.

I hit his jaw with a satisfying crack, then throw my head back and slam it against his nose. I ignore his words and his grunts of pain when I hammer my fist into his chest.

I want her back. I need her fucking back here with me where she belongs.

Mine.

I wrap my legs around his body and use them to throw him off me, quickly jumping to my feet. I rush toward the corridor, but Cole stands there, his eyes mirroring mine, fierce with rage.

I spit blood from my mouth.

"What the fuck are you doing, Rage?" He glares at me like I'm a psychopath, his eyebrows furrowing in confusion.

"He doesn't know, Rage. He doesn't know." I can sense Lucas standing behind me, but his words do little to relax me.

"Get the fuck away from the door!"

Cole ignores me. Instead, he looks over my shoulder at Lucas, asking, "Doesn't know what?"

"I said. Get. The. Fuck. Away. From. The. Door." My voice gets deadlier on each word.

"Doesn't know fucking what?" Cole's unraveling. Even I can sense it in my state.

"It's her." Lucas's words sound broken even to my unapologetic ears. I refuse to listen to anything other than the whimpers behind the door.

"Her?"

My fists ball tighter, the blood from my knuckles dripping to the floor.

"Tia."

My head spins back in Lucas's direction. "That's not her fucking name!"

He licks his cracked lip. "It's her name now, brother."

The tight band around my last bit of self-control snaps, and I lunge for him once again, slamming him up against the wall with such force the plaster cracks.

Cole's arm tightens around my neck in a choke hold, but I refuse to give in. I refuse to release the bastard who betrayed me.

"Enough, Rage. Enough!" Cole tugs me back harder, but I let my fingers grip Lucas's neck tighter. I'm acutely aware that he isn't fighting, almost accepting his fate.

His lips begin to turn blue, but my mind is so contorted in rage, I refuse to acknowledge anything other than the red haze surrounding me.

I hate him so much.

"Her name's Thalia. She's mine." I whimper lowly as realization dawns on Cole's devastated face.

I hate them all.

To be continued...

AFTERWORD

HIDDEN IN BRUTAL DEVOTION CONTINUES IN...

LOVE IN BRUTAL DEVOTION

Available to Pre-order here: LOVE IN BRUTAL DEVOTION

Would you like a sneak peek of what's to come?
Sign up to BJ Alpha's newsletter for an exclusive look at
Love In Brutal Devotion and be the first to hear about
BJ's up-and-coming events and book news.

Use the link to get a sneak peek now:
Sneak peek of Love In Brutal Devotion

ACKNOWLEDGMENTS

1 year on and seven books later!
Tee the lady that started it all for me.
Thank you so much.

I must start with where it all began, TL Swan. When I started reading your books, I never realized I was in a place I needed pulling out of. Your stories brought me back to myself.

With your constant support and the network created as 'Cygnet Inkers' I was able to create something I never realized was possible, I genuinely thought I'd had my day. You made me realize tomorrow is just the beginning.

To Kate, thank you for everything. I'm so grateful to have you by my side both in the book world and on a friendship level.

Emma H, thank you for your daily messages and always being there for me.

Thank you to my friends Julie and Hayden for being my biggest cheerleaders. I appreciate you both.

Martina Dale, thank you for your support as always.

Jenn and Tash thank you ladies for all your support and photos, you really know how to brighten up my day.

To the ladies in **Cygnets** you girls are amazing. I wish you the all best and every success.

Swan Squad
Thank you Tee for bringing these amazing ladies into my life all through the love of books.
A special thank you to our girls;
Bren, Sharon H, Patricia, Caroline, Claire, Anita, Sue and Mary-Anne.

Beta Readers
Thank you to my Beta Readers for your continual support.
Libby, Jaclyn, Kate and Savannah.

ARC Team
To my ARC readers thank you.
I have such an amazing team and I need you all to know that I appreciate each and every message, share, graphic and review.
Thank you so much.

To my world.
To my boys reach high and dream big the world is yours for the taking. Be true to yourself and embrace every minute. I'm proud of you both.
Be happy.

To my hubby, the J in my BJ.
Thank you for holding me up when I'm down.
You're the best
Love you trillions!

About the Author

BJ Alpha lives in the UK with her hubby, two teenage sons and three fur babies.
She loves to write and read about hot, alpha males and feisty females.

Follow me on my social media pages:
Facebook: BJ Alpha
My readers group: BJ's Reckless Readers
Instagram: BJ Alpha

ALSO BY B J ALPHA

Secrets and Lies Series

CAL Book 1

CON Book 2

FINN Book 3

BREN Book 4

OSCAR BOOK 5

Born Series

Born Reckless

PRE-ORDER NOW!

LOVE IN BRUTAL DEVOTION

(The Brutal Duet Book 2)

Printed in Great Britain
by Amazon

19751110R00163